Praise for
When We Were Murderous Time-Traveling Women

Ellen Morris Prewitt has created a unique story that will surprise from the very first page. In rich, descriptive language, the author delivers a whirlwind adventure that unfolds in enchanting New Orleans. There are plenty of plot twists, and rest assured expectations will be subverted. But it's the drawing of the characters that holds much of the novel's humor and warmth. Oh, and how awesome our grannies are, especially the murderous ones.
—Gordon Haynes, author of *Catching Souls for Beelzebub*

The magic and majesty of New Orleans is on full display in this brilliant piece that weaves intrigue, ancestral magic, and acceptance of our own checkered histories. The blend of past and present woven with beautiful prose is spellbinding, and holds you close from start to finish.
—J. D. Marcey, author of *Exodus Missed*

I love everything about this book. I want to eat it with a spoon.
—Marisa Whitsett Baker, avid reader and former bookseller

When We Were Murderous Time Traveling Women

Ellen Morris Prewitt

Literary Wanderlust | Denver, Colorado

When We Were Murderous: Time Traveling Women is a work of fiction. Names, characters, places and incidents are either the product of the author's imagination or are used fictitiously, and any resemblance to actual persons, living or dead, business establishments, event or locales is entirely coincidental.

Copyright © 2026 by Ellen Morris Prewitt

All rights reserved. No part of this publication may be reproduced, distributed, stored in a retrieval system, or transmitted in any form or by any means, including photocopying, recording, or other electronic or mechanical methods, without the prior written permission of the publisher, except in the case of brief quotations embodied in critical reviews and certain other noncommercial uses permitted by copyright law.

Published in the United States by Literary Wanderlust LLC, Denver, Colorado. www.LiteraryWanderlust.com

ISBN print: 978-1-956615-62-3
ISBN digital: 978-1-956615-63-0

Author's Note

The story explores the impact of being forced to kill. Trauma—such as amputation, rape, difficult childbirth, suicide, bullying, and alcohol abuse—impacts the characters, as do their reactions to the trauma. Though violence primarily takes place off-page, the topic and the telling might be disturbing, including the absurdist tone used to deflect the trauma. Please know this—no animals die, except a small brown mouse and a possum who deserved it.

"Virgie had reached the point where in the next moment she might turn into something without feeling it shock her."
Eudora Welty, "The Wanderers" in *Golden Apples*

*To all the women who birthed me
and the men who
did not
bring violence into their lives.*

Part I

The Setup

Chapter 1

"Ancient Chartres decree the Royal Dauphine drink Burgundy while seated on the Rampart of the castle until St. Claude rises from the dead, again."

Oblivious to the danger, I recited the ditty I had made up to keep myself on track as I wove toward Bywater Coffee, hoping the owners hadn't randomly decided to close early like they sometimes did. At the time, I had no idea ditties shouldn't be created, much less recited, in susceptible New Orleans. What I'm saying, it was ignorance, not adventure, that brought me up short at the base of a stone castle on Royal Street. Neck craned against the sunlight slanting from Chartres Street to St. Claude Avenue, I struggled to decide if that was truly a velvet-clad prince lounging on the castle's rampart while swigging from a bottle of cheap red wine.

I could claim I was shocked to see the heavy gray castle with its jutting rampart, but I'd be lying. And I'm trying to tell this story straight, which is so, so hard to do because who understands something the first time it happens? Truth is, I had been making up shit since I fled my first Mississippi killing. (First, you might ask, but the women in my family never seem to stop at one.) "Aurora Etoile," I would say when introducing myself. "I go by my last name." Lonely and desperate to sound French and exotic, because everyone knows New Orleans respects the exotic. What I didn't get was that the city respects the *authentic* exotic and could distinguish that from a poser as naturally as hot air rising creates a breeze, a wind, then a tearing hurricane. Now I had conjured a castle.

The situation on the rampart had turned precarious. The guy groaned and slung a leg over the edge. The leg was clad in blue velvet knickers, white stockings below. Wavy black curls kissed the collar of his gold-laced cape. He coughed, pitiful, as if he were on his way out of this world. The leaves of a giant maple crowding the castle fluttered, exposing their silvery undersides. For a moment, I thought the webs woven in its branches intended to cradle the guy in case he over-lolled, but that was just magical thinking. Below the rampart, the tree roots thrust the sidewalk into a pointy, dangerous palisade.

I opened my mouth to call out, to warn him he was getting too close to the edge, but St. Claude appeared, his pleated linen robe billowing against the orange clouds of the setting sun.

The dauphine (because by then I realized what I'd done) set down his half-empty bottle of burgundy. His red-stained lips parted as he stared at the Jesuit priest descending gently onto the wide rampart. When St. Claude's black silk slippers scraped the stone, his gaze traveled from the dauphine to me.

The son of a king burped.

St. Claude locked his gaze onto the dauphine. The once-dead-alive-again saint knitted his plucked eyebrows. Claude de la Colombière. Priest, writer, and confessor known for his mystical visions, or so said a brass plaque on his street. Mostly famous for being the spiritual director to some nun, which probably meant spending hours closeted in the same wooden room where he slipped on—and off—his scratchy linen vestments, hot confessions mixing. None of that simple life for him now. His lace-trimmed robe hung heavy with seed pearls. It caught the orange sun and glowed, aflame. He crinkled his nose in disgust at the supine dauphine.

With a groan, the dauphine leaned over the rampart and spewed ruby vomit.

See? We can always feel others judging us.

"Hey!" I yelled at the saint, mad at him for bullying the vulnerable dauphine. "What do you think you're doing?"

The saint swiveled his head to me. "Are you ready?" he asked, his English tinged with a French-lilt but otherwise perfect. "The time has come to declare yourself. Are you in, or are you out?"

"Oh, I'm in." Who knows what he meant, but damn if I'd be cut out of my own vision.

"Then you must choose, *mon petit chou chou.*"

Choices. I hated being forced to choose. *You can't make me* rose from my inner petulant child.

The sainted-one must have seen my stubbornness because he said, "You cannot conjure then refuse to play that which you have set in motion." He picked something off his robe, which looked immaculate to me, but who was I to question the standards of a saint. "You've been granted a familiar to help you perform the needed task, but only one. All three of these women cannot come with you."

My heart leaped—three women? Could it be?

"No way," I said. "If you mean who I think you mean, they're all mine."

"You choose even when you think you do not." St. Claude lifted his palms as if to call forth every demon ever said to inhabit the most libeled city in America. His toes rose off the rampart. The sun behind him flashed blood red.

The dauphine struggled onto one elbow and croaked, "Wait."

Too late. I was no longer on the sidewalk. I was no longer in charge of my bodily comings and goings.

I was inside the castle.

Chapter 2

The castle's dark foyer stunk so bad I almost gagged—rat turds, wet mold, and what? Glue? Or dough popping yeast bubbles in a bowl in the kitchen? The castle door slowly contracted behind me, and I laughed out loud. What the hell? Had I landed in a Scooby Doo movie?

I glanced over my shoulder. No one was there. Oddly enough, I could see through the door's mullioned windows all the way to the end of cobblestoned Montegut Street. Montegut dead-ended at three palm trees. Then the wall protecting the city against an overflow of the Mississippi River. The metal fin of an oil tanker glided above the concrete flood wall. I was looking up at the fin, up at the river, up.

The fin glided out of sight.

As my eyes adjusted to the dark, the last ray of light I might ever see caught on a suit of armor and glanced me a blow. I stepped to the side for a better view.

Three staircases rose in front of me. One swept to the left, one to the right. A final one led straight up to a landing backed by a stained glass window. At the foot of each staircase stood my three ancestral grannies. Not my own grannies, the women who had raised me and deeded me purpose and bestowed their illicit gifts on me. Forced them upon me, actually. No, these women on the staircase were the beginnings of me, the first of each line. They were already real to me, though, through the stories my grannies had told little-girl me. Tip-Top. Bigmama. Elfy.

Each with her own peculiar talent represented an unspoken choice to take with me to the dauphine. (The e, I know—it's a problem, but I was oblivious at this point, so I can't explain it to you yet.)

"Assess and pick one," said the voice of the saint.

I could have predicted this. Even when I was tearing away from Mississippi, guilt snapping at my heels, I knew one day I would be forced to choose something besides a fancy fake name.

"The dauphine awaits, Etoile."

"Claude," I began, but Tip-Top's steady stare stopped me. Like she flat-out knew I had run away from her beloved Mississippi. But if she understood the whole story, she'd forgive me, right?

"There," said the saint. "Start there. And do it quickly. That boy won't stay on the rampart forever."

Chapter 3

All bad things start in Alabama. That's not talking ugly. It's a geographical fact. Alabama is a sinkhole that burps onion-tinged gas. The earth spins, and the gas rolls east toward the Atlantic, helped along by the puffed cheeks of easily offended Mississippi.

At least that was the story my Tippy told me when I was young enough to yawn at eight o'clock in the evening, worn out from a day of riding horses and running from the mean-ass geese who claimed the barn as their own soon as the weather turned cool. We would be in Tippy's bedroom, my Tippy and me. She sat on the edge of the bed with its popcorn bedspread slipping to the floor, its weight pulled sideways by the dense quilts she took to sewing and layering on the bed after her long-ago husband left her for a woman in Mobile. Only much later did I realize this might have been the source of Tippy's take on Alabama. At the time, I wondered why my granny, who flipped the lawn mower on its side to clean clumped grass from its steel blades and changed her own flat whenever a tire picked up a nail, had such a dainty hobby as quilting. When I had asked her this, she sat me down at the sewing machine, and pressing the foot pedal, made me watch the slick needle whir up and down, up and down, piercing the fabric with tiny, effective holes. "Listen carefully, child. You can find satisfaction anywhere."

Tippy's bedroom smelled tangy like Bengay and—because I stayed with Tippy in the winter when gas heaters hissed—scorched dust. I sprawled on the bed in my flannel nightgown, my stomach full of the salty boiled peanuts Tippy set aside for my snack, while we watched TV before bed. I sucked on a slick strand of my hair. On the bedroom dresser, the black oscillating fan Tippy never turned off whirred while she talked trash about Alabama, my favorite thing.

Mississippi was way better than Alabama, Tippy assured me as she plaited her hair into a braid thick as a water moccasin. Along her forehead and temples, her black hair shaded to gray and curved like a tiara. When she looped her braid over her head, the tiara became a full-blown crown.

"How much better is Mississippi?" I asked, rising to fetch the silver-backed mirror with the tarnished mermaid riding a wave on the sea.

"We could beat Alabama with one hand tied behind our back," she replied, examining the neatness of her handwork in the angled mirror. "Fair fight. No Alabama-cheat-'em rules." She flipped her plait over her shoulder and squinted at me to make sure I absorbed her point. "Alabama is good for nothing but running away from."

The bedtime tales Tippy told me weren't exactly an origin story, but she did get them from her great-grandmother Tip-Top, the first of that line, the tippy top of the Tippy heap. Tip-Top was Cherokee.

Please be clear about this. I might be a gentrifying jerk who steals atmosphere for her stories, but I am not claiming I am Cherokee. I was raised a white-bread child of two alcoholic parents whose one act of kindness was farming me out to my various grandmothers for care. I went to Tippy's farm in the winter because she would see that I got to school. In the summers, my other grandmother and great-grandmother hosted me at their mansion in Jackson because they had ceiling fans. (I didn't make these decisions.) I am poor White trash. Poor enough to enjoy commodity cheese. White enough to have my crazy Jackson grandmothers called eccentric. Trashy enough to sweat on Tippy's upholstered couch on her front porch. If there is such a thing as White, I am it.

Tip-Top was born in Georgia in 1824, right before the Georgia gold rush shot off. When that happened, Tip-Top's life changed with no warning. One day, the four-year-old was seated in the grass watching her mama clean the sharp blade on an iron plow, and the next day she and Dancing Water were on the move. The family landed in Lookout Mountain, Alabama. Sounds quaint, but think of it this way: *Lookout!*

The White man who accompanied Dancing Water on the trek was in the army. What army? A remnant of the Revolutionary militia? Or the army that was running Dancing Water's Cherokee tribe out of Georgia so White settlers could steal the tribe's gold? This type of detail gets lost when a story is flattened to its essence: Tip-Top was the child of Dancing Water who left Georgia with a White army man. The makeshift family settled on tribal land, which was why Tippy declared, as she brushed her silvery hair until it sparked, we had never been from Alabama. Tippy had life beginning and ending where she wanted it.

Here's the tricky part. Dancing Water thought she was protecting her daughter from greedy White men, but the Trail of Tears loomed on the horizon. In the lead-up to the forced removal, the White people began agitating. I don't know exactly what happened in those years, and Tippy would never elaborate to a youngster like me, but I gathered beautiful young Tip-Top had too many "suitors." Ill-suited suitors. Aggressive suitors. When Tip-Top was fourteen, the family kept moving west.

Quickly. They loaded their possessions into an oxcart and trundled from northeast Alabama to the black, fecund dirt of the Mississippi Delta.

Except, apparently, my poor sense of direction was already embedded in our genes back then. The tiny family drifted off course. Wound up in the southwest section of the southwest territory of Mississippi. Not the fertile Delta, but the forests of the Piney Woods. Pine away, you ain't gonna get rich in the Piney Woods. The Native Americans living there were Choctaw, and my Tippy said therein lay the confusion in our family tree. We were of Cherokee heritage, but the memory got crosshatched with the real presence of the Choctaw tribe in the land where Tip-Top married, buried three miscarried fetuses, birthed one healthy son, survived the Civil War, and lost her right foot to a bear trap before said son cajoled her onto the stage where she was killed. Her husband's name—I kid you not—was John Smith.

I'm sure Smith was a criminal absconding to Mississippi to escape prosecution. Hence his alias. No one talks about it.

Anyway, it doesn't matter. (But surely you can see why I needed Etoile? I mean, Smith.) The point is, nothing about me is connected to the males in my heritage. All of me, along that strand goes back to Tip-Top, who arrived in Mississippi in a mad dash. She would set the tone for every female that would come down her line, including me. She killed. I'm not saying she was so good-looking she slayed men. I'm talking immaculately-cleaned knives. Once in self-defense. Once accidentally. And once, back in *Lookout!*, solely because the aggressive son of a bitch deserved killing. Or as Tippy would whisper when the sag in the mattress rolled me next to her until I awoke nearly suffocating from my mouth pressed against her shoulder, gasping for air like a dying sucker fish, "Killing is sometimes the only option left a woman."

Tip-Top was the ancestor standing at the foot of the left staircase.

Chapter 4

A song strummed down the staircases, splitting at the top and rolling off the walls in a reverberating one-man chorus. The dauphine, singing on the rampart. Not in drunken bawdiness. A lament. He had a beautiful voice. The notes rose and fell. The boy had quite the range. I started toward the stairs.

That was one of my choices. March right past the three women guarding the staircases and wind my way up to the dauphine. Hang out on the rampart with him, sharing his burgundy, as the silken night fell. Forget about preachy-judgy St. Claude with his nice threads and will-of-God devotion and really just all of the nonsense that made me conjure him in the first place.

As if called by name, the saint appeared on the landing. He perched his butt on the edge of the marble console, hands clasped at his knees.

"Etoile?" he asked, and I could have kissed him for using my made-up name.

"Yes, Claude?"

"Are you telling them about your ancestors?"

"Yes, Claude."

"The truth?"

"As I know it."

"Don't fudge." He produced a peach from the folds of his magnificent robe and bit. Peach juice sluiced down his chin. He flicked it off before it splattered his robe. "And what about you? Are you telling the truth about your own life?"

"I'm working up to it."

"Dropping hints?"

I nodded, because while I have not told you about the evening I lay in the grass beneath the rattling pecan leaves and formulated a murderous plan while the needlelike proboscis of a mosquito I could not swat away drew blood from my cheek, I have told you my Tip-Top gifted me with an understanding of necessary killing.

"You better make it quick." St. Claude nodded over his shoulder. "He's serious up there."

"What's his problem?" I asked because even though I had obviously conjured him, not everything conjured in New Orleans arrives as planned. I expected the Bywater had assented to my subconscious dreaming for reasons purely its own.

The saint sighed. "I failed, that is his problem. It was my job as his tutor to feed him that pap about the holy emissary destined to rule, the burden of the crown as a suffering that is pleasing to God, blah, blah, blah. He refuses, as he puts it, to 'play the game.' He's very dramatic, the dear boy, and exaggerates the danger of the situation. You might be able to convince him, if not to reign, at least not to take his own life. Or"—he flipped his palm back and forth in a who-knows gesture—"you might not. But you won't get the chance if you don't hurry."

At the risk of his telling me exactly what he thought of me— the worst kind of poser, the observing, sarcastic kind—I asked,

"Why me? Why do you think I have sympathy for a rich kid heir to the throne?"

He chomped into the peach. The sound of his chewing echoed off the stone walls. Licking his lips, he said, "I don't. In fact, I think you might want to see him dead. But I don't want to prejudge. Point is, his decision is nearing, and if his choice goes bad, like the cetacean he's named for, he'll arch into the air, and two stories is high when your landing is spotted with chunks of stone."

A woman's derisive snort filled the air. "Talk about purple prose."

I glanced at my ancestor standing at the foot of the middle staircase. The first Bigmama, tall as a redwood. I'd seen her photo on the back cover of her books. The library had two titles on its shelves. I'd bought another three from a company in India that printed out-of-copyright books. I couldn't stomach reading more after that.

The dull thrum of an overhead helicopter vibrated the castle windows. Army, no doubt. The damn things circled all the time. Echoed by St. Claude's fingers drumming a Devil's tattoo on the marble console.

Better pick up the pace.

Chapter 5

The first Bigmama did not believe babies were a blessing. She considered them a danger, a threat, an often-fatal condition to be avoided if at all possible. She felt this way for the same reason we all have opinions: life had taught her the truth of it. She put off the danger of birth as long as possible until she and the city of Vicksburg surrendered together.

When the United States Army of the American Civil War attacked the river city, Bigmama spent months ignoring the thud of cannonballs as she baked biscuits, drew cool water from the cistern, and watched the moss slowly cover the brick-lined path to the stables. Occasionally, she looked up to see the ships positioning their guns, sighting for the living room. At that moment, the deep front porch seemed too shallow. It was. The cannon ball holes splintering the wood proved that.

Tired of wasting shot, in May of 1863, the Yankees began the siege. As Federal troops blockaded the town, the Confederates dug caves in the hills, and Bigmama and her sister citizens waltzed from their homes into the protective caves, dragging their platform rockers and turtle-top tables and flame mahogany secretaries behind them.

Nine months later, at the age of forty-six, Bigmama lay alone on her full-tester bed in her ravaged home. The balls of her feet pressed the footboard, her clenched jaw cut off the cry of labor. When the infant arrived, Bigmama severed her own umbilical cord, rose from the bed, and lit the wood stacked in the fireplace to heat water for cleaning the infant. Turning from the grate, she crouched, and the placenta slid down her thigh onto the wide-planked floor. The baby let loose her first wail as, across town at the courthouse, Pemberton surrendered to Grant.

Bigmama never disclosed the name of the baby's father, because if her husband had visited her in the cave, it would have been treason. Any other explanation would have been worse. All for naught, as by the time she gave in to the labor pains, the husband was presumed dead, a casualty of the Confederacy's misguided war.

Here, my own Bigmama, who was telling the tale, glared at me—daring me to acknowledge she was almost talking about sex. She jumped ahead to when the golden-haired baby could crawl and thus fend for herself. While the little girl explored unattended, poking her fat thumb into the cannonball divots in the parlor wall, the first Bigmama pulled the cane-bottomed chair from the writing desk, sat, and wrote. For the next nineteen years, she kept herself and her baby alive by writing on and on and on about the Old South.

She penned stories of fluffy white cotton picked by happy enslaved men. Tales of sumptuous sweet potato casseroles served in bone china by happy enslaved women. Narratives of beautiful babies cared for by happy enslaved young girls. Scenes of prancing stallions groomed by happy enslaved little boys.

Her fellow—and sister—Southerners had lived the life. They had wielded the whip, worked the six-year-olds in the hundred-degree heat. They knew the horror. Surely this satirical fairy tale

Bigmama was weaving would make them at least fidget uncomfortably in their chairs.

It did not.

The novels were best sellers. Southerners couldn't get enough of 'em. Northerners lapped them up too, saying, see— we told you we needed to let this go. The checks rolled in, making Bigmama independent in a time when women with young children usually were not. At this point in the telling, my Bigmama would cut her eyes from me, and I knew something was being left out. When I asked why Bigmama kept writing her stories if no one got them, she said, "She wrote the story she wanted to write. Do not blame the writer if her audience are fools."

What I came to understand as an adult was that each time Bigmama lifted her pen, she became more outrageous, more egregious so that, surely this time, readers would see the satires for what they were. She never succeeded, nor did she give up. As a consequence, my first Bigmama single-handedly, through twenty-one execrable novels, created the Southern myth of the Lost Cause where the Old South was noble and brave and only concerned with preserving its genteel way of life. Her engrossing, false, prolific tales supplanted the known violent truth, doing untold damage.

Imagination. That was the gift passed to me from the first Bigmama. Imagination, if not a well-functioning moral compass.

With one exception—when a conceited son-in-law taught his baby girl to say *Grandmère*—every grandmother down that line had been called Bigmama, and each birthed only one child. Just enough to keep the line going but no extraneous risk-taking.

My own Bigmama was the first Bigmama all over again. She had strong, ropey forearms and wore clomping boots—garden boots, rain galoshes, reinforced Redwings. She was my mother's mother, a "widow" after her husband left her while she was away. Through that traitor of a husband, the love-of-alcohol gene entered our family, where it poisoned my mom, who poisoned my dad, leaving both of them unable to properly care for me. But I had my grannies.

While my winters were country nights filled with Tippy's tales, my humid summers meant languid days at Bigmama's mansion. Like Tippy, my Bigmama was obsessed with teaching me my past (you wonder where I got it from). She would recite stories about the first Bigmama in Vicksburg, imprinting her truths by walking me in circles in her backyard garden.

My Bigmama liked walking in circles in the yard.

It reminded her of the only comfort she had in prison.

I would tell you my granny was framed. That she didn't actually libel half of Jackson with her scurrilous letters to the editor, but I suspect that somehow, some way, the saint is listening to what I tell you. Unfortunately, one of her letters to the editor libeled the mayor in a way that instigated violence. Extreme violence, which led the city attorney into creative prosecution for incitement. In her defense, my Bigmama channeled the first Bigmama and claimed the mayor deserved to have the truth told about him, even if she had to make up a lie to do it.

Bigmama learned her lesson. Libel requires publication. When she was released from the dark cell back into the light, she stayed away from the newspaper. She didn't quit writing. Like the first Bigmama's retreat into fantasy after her time in the dank caves, my Bigmama went underground.

Each morning, after Bigmama clattered her oatmeal bowl into the sink for Elfy to clean, she pried a spiral-bound notebook from the stuffed kitchen drawer. Seated ramrod at the Formica table, she wrote letter after letter. Some went to childhood friends she perceived as having done her wrong. Some went to companies offering shoddy service. The one she leaned into hard enough to tear the paper went to a little boy in my Sunday school class who shoved me against the wall for beating him in a Bible drill. In each letter, she told the truth of the harm done . . . exaggerated a bit. When she was finished creating, she tore the letters from her notebook with a rippppp, cleaned off the dangling paper strands, and stuffed the folded missives in gold-lined envelopes scrolled with her monogram. Vitriol wrapped in beauty.

As she wrote, I played in the backyard with the stray kittens who appeared every summer. I caught lizards among the bitter-smelling geraniums and, with a rippppp, cleaned off their tails to see if they really would grow back. I cawed to the crow, flapping my wings while it sat impassive, beady eye unwavering. After Bigmama left her daily dose of correspondence for the mail carrier to pick up, we were ready for my daily dose of family history as we walked the yard. Then I was happy. The sweat trickled between my shoulder blades. Hot, it was always hot when I stayed at Bigmama's. At her house, I had someone to hold my hand. I had daring tales of strength and perseverance and the will to survive. I felt destined.

So yeah, from my two ancestors—Tip-Top on the left staircase and Bigmama in the middle—I've been given an understanding of the need to kill and an imagination with no morals.

That's two out of the three, which, as they say, ain't bad.

Chapter 6

St. Claude lifted his palms from the marble-top table and slow clapped. My chest warmed, pleased to have impressed him.

Then he glanced at the dimming day, calculating time. "You have one left, Etoile. Make it quick. Which ancestor will you take with you to confront the dauphine?"

I didn't like it, him forcing my hand. It didn't bode well in this fleur-de-lis city where everything arrives in a trinity. Bad enough I was in the foyer of a make-believe castle on the road from Chartres (Char-ters, by the way) to Dauphine (Daw-pheen) via Royal onto Burgundy (Bur-GUN-dy) to Rampart before hitting St. Claude (Saint Clawd). I could easily have been three blocks over where Piety invariably flames Desire which leads to illicit Congress before forever squelching Independence. Don't fuck with this city. Its wisdom is written in asphalt, its imagination drawn in the graffiti that bloomed from Katrina mold. Its secrets hide in lodges, closed societies, and—now—conjured castles.

I feared the city was trying to teach me a lesson: If I thought I could play the city, I would be the one played. My pretender-self waltzing over from Mississippi would be exposed. A castle would appear at the end of my stroll, and a saint would twist my arm until I was forced to choose which of my ancestors I would take to the knife fight that is life.

All right. Here she is, my third, and most conniving ancestor, Elfy.

Chapter 7

My Elfy was plump as a pin cushion. She spoke in spurts, nibbling her fingers between her words. She was my great-grandmother and lived in the mansion with my Bigmama, who was her daughter-in-law. Elfy tended the house, always polishing and dusting. Much, much later in life, I realized all that spiffing and fussing was channeling unmet sexual desire, a conclusion confirmed on this quest as I got to know the first Elfy. But I'm getting ahead of myself.

My Elfy rose late in the day after Bigmama had finished at the kitchen table (I think she wanted deniability) and ate half a cantaloupe followed by sausage patties fried in the iron skillet then lace-edged pancakes cooked in the leftover grease. Each day she designated a room for cleaning. I followed in her wake while she worked, and she told me of the first Elfy, whose portrait hung on the dining room wall.

Our first Elfy married a man named Gerald Morris. Gerald was best friends with the man married to Elfy's sister. Well, the best friend the man had made since he dragged Elfy's sister from refined Richmond to the new raw state of Mississippi. The Magnolia State, which was then the Wild West, must not have had many women, because Gerald hit up his friend to introduce him to the wife's sister. After Elfy's sister gave her stamp of approval, Elfy consented to letting Gerald visit her in Richmond.

Gerald came off well. He was a blacksmith turned jeweler who'd been elected to the Jackson City Council (yes, they had politics in the mid-nineteenth century). Gerald was going places in that foreign land of Mississippi, and unlike most men who escaped to the territory to start over, Gerald came from a good, if Northern, family. So Elfy accepted Gerald's marriage proposal and relocated to the state her sister had three years earlier adopted as her own.

Best-friend sisters marrying best-friend men. Elfy shouldn't have done it. Never, ever try to mirror anything. The universe will break your jaw every time for that cutesy shit.

Though doctors warned Elfy that, at less than five feet tall, she was too diminutive to bear children, within a year of marriage, her first child arrived. The kids came regularly after that. Elfy adored them, every one, as she did Gerald. Under his tutelage, she learned to etch the delicate initials his wealthy jewelry clients preferred for their lockets and flasks. She began to keep the business's books and taught herself calligraphy to write the sums into the ledgers. "Everything deserves to be floweredy," was her motto.

Five years into the marriage, the winds of Civil War blew unrest into Mississippi. Elfy didn't care. She was busy at her lovely home, which fronted the most prestigious street in town, trendy Empire furniture gracing its rooms, prisms dancing rainbows across Persian rugs. Elfy's offspring had bloomed to four with a fifth three weeks from entering the world when Gerald chose to leave his pregnant wife and return to his native North for a visit and die.

Nothing shocking there. Sudden death happened then,

same as it does now. Unfortunately, though, the news of Gerald's death arrived as Elfy's labor pains crescendoed (you see why the women in my family view babies as a crapshoot). The child was stillborn. Elfy named her Dolores, because Elfy was truly a sad lady. She dragged that sorrow behind her as she prepared the house for the double wake, expecting her husband's body to return home any day. Instead, her brother-in-law bustled in waving a sheet of paper. Letters. Not the kind you write. The kind a court issues.

Gerald's father had filed a will that purported to disinherit Elfy and her offspring. The father disparaged Gerald's wife and children in Mississippi as interlopers threatening to cheat his son's "God-ordained" family. Worse, he kept his son's body, already in a cold grave in the foreign North.

When Elfy understood from the fancy language that the forces of darkness—to wit, her scheming father-in-law—had betrayed her, her rage boiled. Seems Gerald's "good family," like many, had fallen on hard times. Her rapacious father-in-law coveted the jewelry business, the inventory of the shop, even the monogrammed forks in the silver chest. Oh, Elfy could see the evil man whispering in the ear of dying Gerald, his breath rancid from the sassafras root he chewed, insisting those down in Mississippi didn't count as real family, badgering Gerald until he executed a new will.

New will. Thank you, blessed baby Jesus, for that meant during Gerald's sane years in Mississippi, he had executed a prior will. Elfy corralled her brother-in-law after baby Dolores's funeral and pressed the true will into his hands. Tears welled in her eyes, her delicate chin trembled, but her shoulders were set, determined to overcome her utter helplessness. Thoroughly affected, her brother-in-law agreed to challenge the father's upstart will in court. He would see to it that Elfy's babies reaped the benefit of their father's hard work. He would defeat the

Devil who was hurling brimstone onto their heads from the conniving, greedy North.

The brother-in-law never looked at the will closely enough to see the ink so newly smudged on the page. Nor did he compare the sweeping calligraphy of Gerald's declaration with the fancy entries in the jeweler's ledgers. He refused to admit the rose scent of the linen paper—why would a man's paper carry the scent of a woman? He bought it hook, line, and sinker.

As Elfy and I cleaned and polished the lovely things the first Elfy's guile had ensured stayed in the family, we hashed and rehashed this story. Why did the weak Gerald give in to his father? Why had he left home when his wife was so close to having her baby? Elfy wondered aloud as she curved her chambray cloth over the marble bust of Joan of Arc that had returned from a long-ago trip to France. Why did the brother-in-law go along with the deception of the old will? Did maybe he like Elfy better than her sister? All week, we dusted off furniture and theories. On Sundays, we rested from the cleaning and moved on to implements.

Elfy would jiggle open the drawer of the silver chest and show me the first Elfy's engraving tool with the mushroom cap shaped to give a good grip. She let me brandish the sterling calligraphy pen with its slick mother-of-pearl handle and urged me to trace my finger along the shimmering dragon carved there. She led me upstairs and kneeled before the long drawer in the bottom of the hall wardrobe, where a stash of notepaper with curled-brown corners expired its rose scent. "Even the most delicate item can be deadly," she murmured as I kneeled beside her. My pudgy Elfy wanted me to understand the tools of a woman's trade: a level head, a willingness to fight, and most important, an appreciation of feminine deceit when necessary to ensure the good won.

Never once in that long line of Elfys did good mean anything other than exactly what each Elfy wanted. What they desired—despite any evidence to the contrary—was never evil.

Yes, I am poor White trash. I am also wealthy from the machinations of my long-ago Elfy to save the family fortune from her dastardly father-in-law. In Mississippi, if you didn't admit your family was poor White trash at some point, you were lying.

Chapter 8

The saint cleared his throat, urging me to get on with it. Outside the windows flanking the heavy front door, a tourist tripped on the jagged sidewalk, sending his tall jester's hat flying. I yearned for my tourist bingo card. I'd been needing one of the green/purple/gold hats. I won last October's witch hat bingo and got a twenty-five dollar gift certificate to Bywater Coffee. Happy days.

You don't know what the saint meant me to get on with.

I knew.

My story. He wanted me to tell you my story. The hardest thing of all.

Here goes. I should've been suspicious when the president of the most prestigious ad agency in Jackson offered me and my associate degree a job. At the time, I attributed it to affirmative action, Mississippi-style: "I'll take White Female Community College Grad for one hundred dollars, Alex." Plus, a part of me shamefully hoped he respected my family's tattered reputation. My Elfy had been somebody before she and her ex-felon daughter-in-law became the city's bat-shit-crazy old ladies.

That type of self-delusion landed me tussling in the grass under a pecan tree, fighting the man who had championed me since the day I slid my resume onto his shiny ebony desk. I didn't stand a chance one-on-one with him. He had me by at least one hundred and twenty pounds, plus his two fully functioning feet. My face wound up smashed into the grass, my nose filled with the stink of green pecan shells. My arms were pinned and unable to slap the mosquito steadily drawing blood from my poor cheek.

As the horror of what was happening became real, I saw the facts that should have sparked outrage in a different light. He had mentored me for two years, invited me to his house for dinner, gave me plum assignments that showed he believed in me professionally. These would be twisted and used against me. I had brought this on myself, they would say. I owed him. Surely I understood payment would be taken.

In that moment of most need, I forgot everything my grannies had taught me. I stopped thrashing. The movement might catch a party-goer's attention. They wouldn't call out or come to my rescue, but so help me God, if something untoward ever happened to the asshole, the intentionally-blind would reluctantly go to the police and report their suspicions of what they thought they had seen under the pecan tree at the firm party.

I never again ate pecans. I did get my justice.

You're wanting details. Maybe a gory story about a late night at the office, a garbage sack for protection against spattered blood, a carefully planned and methodically executed killing. But I'm not into revenge porn.

I kept working for him (to pay the rent) and dutifully went to his office when he called, even if it was after everyone had gone home (as I said, it was my job). As he leaned over my proposed draft of a cat food campaign, his hand wandered to the waistband of my skirt where it found bare skin.

Instinctively, I used the move I'd learned in every self-defense course I'd ever taken (don't incessantly teach women self-defense if you don't expect us to use it). I pressed into him with my buttocks, then, hard as I could, elbowed upward toward his jaw. The blow knocked him against the wall. Except between him and the wall was the shelf displaying his do-gooder awards, including the Addy the firm had won for a particularly successful dental hygiene campaign.

All I can figure, my initial shove must have wobbled the crystal obelisk. My second shove—more emphatic—impaled him against the trophy's pointy top. The makeshift dagger entered his back with the squishy sound of sugarcane: a fibrous, juicy noise. He slid down the wall. I hadn't touched him, hadn't touched the obelisk. He looked pretty dead to me, wide-eyed on the floor, but I didn't check his pulse. I figured if he were alive and survived until the cleaning crew arrived, so be it. He could squeal on me, and I'd take my lumps. But if the universe wanted him to die, I wasn't going to involve myself in that. I left for the evening and kept my mouth shut during the hysteria that followed when his terrified partners believed jealous advertising competitors were out to kill them all, ala *Murder, She Wrote*.

As soon as no one would connect my departure with his demise, I ran.

These are the three gifts I inherited from the women standing at the bottom of the staircase.

From Tip-Top in her deerskin jacket snugged with a heavy leather belt: a respect for the need to kill.

From Bigmama in her white-collared, flat-chested, black watered-silk dress: imagination without morals.

From Elfy in her green hoop skirt with its girlish petticoat: the barbed wire of feminine deceit wrapped in crinoline.

Three women, all living in the wilds of the new American Southwest, all killed on the same Wednesday in 1873.

Gems, each of them. I hit the trifecta with my ancestral

grannies. Yet, the sanctimonious St. Claude expected me to pick only one. To choose between these priceless women to journey up the stairs to confront and/or save the dauphine.

To hell with that. Until you prove to me that the world fights fair with women, I won't be following any man's made-up rules.

"I'm taking all three," I said, my answer reverberating through the castle's empty foyer.

Chapter 9

This is what my Bigmama taught me about storytelling: Talking about the past is easy. The past is done. Your only choice as the storyteller is where to start. To do that, pick through the events and select the one that makes the story funny or sad or ironic, then string the rest of the events together so your story finishes with a flourish.

"What's a flourish?" I had asked as we circled the backyard.

"The black eye you gave that Prather boy for talking bad about your mama," she said, gripping my hand.

Telling the future is the same but opposite. Tell it as if it begins from where you stand (everything coming after you is the future) and make up some hooey that renders the beginning funny or sad or ironic or all three. "Like me predicting the mayor's sworn enemies were gonna use that rat poison to kill their rat-faced opponent," she gave by way of example.

But the present? She never talked about the present, and I don't know what she would say if she did, because there's no beginning or end in the present. No two dots to connect, no crooked lines to draw. Only what's happening right now. You can't take the present and twist it into what you want it to be. Which makes telling it hard, almost to impossible.

When I fled Mississippi, I ran to New Orleans because the city had spent the last few years same as me—rocking a romanticized past until a giant storm rolled in and blew the myth to hell, leaving a shaky grip on the future. Only thing, I landed in the difficult no-man's-land of the present.

No worries.

The city and I would figure this shit out together.

Part II

The Climbing

Chapter 10

Evening was falling. The last light of day hit the floor-to-ceiling stained glass window on the castle landing and spackled my ancestral grannies in jeweled color. The window depicted a dragon toying with red-jumpered knights. Two knights lay on the ground, their necks at odd angles. A third, duly frightened, grasped his broad blade sword in both hands. Down Montegut Street, in the apartment where I paid ungodly rent, no one would be wondering where I was. Not even a dog whining and pawing at the door. I was alone in the world. Whatever happened in this castle was on me.

My three ancestors appraised me. Their presence was a whispered reminder of my own grannies, as if the family line had only so many genes. I felt I knew them, and I did, because story is as strong as reality. They didn't know me, didn't even know an antecedent of me. Yet, their eyes were full of the same gratitude I felt in mine. Love could do that, pass between people for no good reason other than it felt itself present. I basked in the joy of having them all together—even Bigmama and Elfy rarely companioned me jointly—and ignored the frisson between them. Their granny love was directed at me, but when their awareness drifted to each other, what had been a warm hum crackled into static. That was to be expected, given the way they died, but still I should have paid more attention to it.

Bigmama clutched a red leather journal to her breast. She exuded the same stern air that had flowed from my own Bigmama. She offered a curt, "Etoile," and I felt seen, judged, and loved. The first Elfy was as deceptively demure as my Elfy but young with a cascade of black curls, pert nose, and liquid brown eyes. She pressed her slim palms against her diaphragm and murmured, "Etoile." Last, Tip-Top. She worked her mouth as if she wanted to say something but couldn't decide exactly what. Her good foot rested on the crewel stair runner. A metal brace ran down her left calf, securing a wooden shoe where the foot should've been. My heart went out to her, to all of them. We were, them and me, a murderous set of Mississippi time-traveling women.

"Time expires." St. Claude scooted off his table and descended in my direction. His ivory robe flowed down the steps like a creamy rill. Old dude smelling of rosewater, huge scarlet cross splashing the front of his robe—this saint did it for me. No hint that his sketchy past with the nun made his religious getup highly suspect. Claim your own truth, that was the ticket.

He nodded as he passed Tip-Top but ignored tiny Elfy and towering Bigmama. As he neared, he motioned for my hand, and I offered it. His palm was dry and sandpapery. I resisted the urge to lick it wet.

"Which will it be?" he asked.

Outside, the train whistle erupted. One, two, three, four long blasts. Through the transom above the arched window, I could make out the steeple of an abandoned Catholic church. The irregular roofscape of my Bywater neighborhood huddled around it. Camelbacks with their one-story fronts rising to two-story additions. Side-by-sides where families lived under one roof separated by a dividing wall. Regular ol' cottages, roofs sprinkled with white crepe myrtle blossoms. So many new roofs, replaced after the storm. The high-ground Bywater hadn't flooded during the hurricane, but lots of houses had suffered then been resurrected. Others, vines climbed the roofs, and, over a decade after the storm, ghosts of spray-painted Xs leftover from the search for bodies haunted the front porches.

You could blame it all on the storm—the shuttering of the church, the cheap No Trespassing signs hanging crooked on the fences, the good cottages transitioning to AirBnBs—but that would be lying. Just like I could blame everything bad in my life on that night under the pecan tree, but in truth it was my response that changed everything.

The saint and I stared at one another, waiting for the train's last long note to evaporate, then he got the drop on me.

"Etoile, I'm not going to insult you. You know how these things work. You are the catalyst, but human angst alone will not break the time barrier. We on our side must desire the fracture. You missed your grannies, as you quaintly call them. We had a task needing completion. These desires came together. In fact, we might have nudged your thoughts in the direction of our desires." He shrugged, a graceful affair. "Regardless, you must make a choice. Who, and which gift, will you take upstairs to the dauphine?"

I slowly withdrew my hand from his. "Are you offering me an incentive? Like my own red jumpsuit, maybe?"

He glanced over his shoulder at the stained-glass window. After a moment of hesitation, he snapped his fingers, and the window scene reversed: The dragon now cowered before the pointed sword of the confident knight. A second snap of the saint's waxy fingers, and I was re-robed. Gone were my artfully torn jeans and cynically profane T-shirt. I was covered in a stretchy red jumpsuit with a broad blade sword hanging from a slinky gold belt. Not bad. The sleeves needed rolling because, even though I'd inherited Bigmama's height, I had Elfy's stubby arms. Still, who could object to the magic bean of a jumpsuit?

"Awesome." I tested the heft of the sword. Or cutlass. Or épée. I have no idea. It was a big-ass knife. Tip-Top stirred, shifting her weight to her good foot. Her wooden shoe was painted a vivid red. It matched my jumpsuit. I took that for a sign.

Fingering the sword's hilt, I repeated, "They all come with me."

Chapter 11

"D'accord," St. Claude said, surprisingly agreeable. He motioned to my ancestors, and they left their posts to gather round. We huddled as close as a football team discussing the next play. I resisted the urge to drape my arms across their shoulders.

"Etoile has an assignment," Claude said, speaking mainly to Tip-Top, and I wondered at his favoritism. His face was long as a pickle, his nose, the warty center. I don't hold that against him. He was, like, 250 years old.

He briefly summarized how we'd gotten here, repeating verbatim the ditty of street names I'd used to conjure the castle. As for summoning my ancestors, he gave himself credit for that. "Etoile is to persuade the dauphine to forgo self-harm and assume the throne as required of him. Rather than following the rules and choosing one of you as her familiar, she insists you all go along."

One by one the grannies turned their gaze on me, teammates waiting for the quarterback to make the call. My stomach lurched. I had never been in charge with my grannies. I was their consistent follower, not the leader. With a trickle of dismay, I realized I had wanted them all to be with me so I could feel again the joy of my childhood—loved, comforted, protected. But I was not a child, and these three clearly saw me as the adult in the room. Woe be unto us.

"One for all," I stupidly said, my voice shaking.

The saint shrugged. "We didn't choose her because she was compliant. But here's the deal: Etoile is a terrible speller."

"Pardon?" While true, it seemed a low blow.

"Etoile believes there is a young man on the rampart about to roll off. The dauphine," St. Claude repeated, and this time he chose Bigmama for his steady gaze.

Bigmama rubbed the front of her journal. Her thumb, crooked as a tree branch, caressed a scene of plantation contentment. "There's an E," she said, her voice hoarse as if she hadn't used it in a while. Clearing her throat, she tried again. "If the person on the rampart is the dauphine, he's not the dauphin. She's the dauphine. With an e."

"Hey!" I objected. "Claude has an e, and he's a guy."

The saint waved his hand through the air. "Different derivation."

"I saw him. Black curls. Deep blue eyes. Classic jaw." I envisioned the young man with his muscular leg slung over the rampart wall. "Trust me, he's a guy."

"He is a vision. Your vision," Claude said. As he talked, he motioned for us to climb the stairs. I swept my arm for my ancestors to go first. I felt more comfortable with them in my sights: Bigmama behind Claude, then Tip-Top, Elfy, and finally me.

At the top of the stairs, the saint led us through a short corridor where we took a sharp right and climbed another set of stairs. The silky singing of whoever was on the rampart trailed down the staircase, leading us on. "The young man is, in fact, you, Etoile, in the sense that every person in a vision—the king on his throne, the maid milking the cow, even the lowing cow—are both who they are and also the author of the vision."

Tip-Top and I paused to wait for Elfy, who had lagged behind. With each step, she halted, pressed her palms and murmured, too low for us to catch the words, then curtsied. I wondered if she were practicing to meet the dauphine. Bigmama trailed her fingers along the stone wall. Examining the resulting soot, she jotted a note in her book. I smiled to myself. It was just like my Bigmama, cooking up a delicious story about our grand adventure.

St. Claude was waiting for me to acknowledge what he'd said. If I understood it, we were parallel, the dauphine and me—his story, my story. Made me wonder who the guy had killed.

Claude turned to face me. The door to the roof was open behind him, and a breeze ruffled his white hair. "The important thing for you to remember as you go forward is that every judgment you cast on him, you cast on yourself."

The unease that had been eating away at the edges of my courage took a big ol' chomp. I pivoted and headed back down the steps. I did not need this psychedelic nonsense in my life. Who in their right mind wanted to deal with a drunken, privileged, cross-gendered embodiment of themselves?

Tip-Top tapped me on the shoulder, and I jumped a mile.

"Keep moving." She nodded upward. Her hair was parted in the middle and pulled into a sleek bun, but she was no Cherokee maiden. In her heavy jacket and canvas pants, she could have been my Tippy dressed for a school play about fur trappers in frontier Mississippi. Her breath came quick, thick, and asthmatic. Or maybe it was her struggling heart. Losing a big chunk of your body—like Tip-Top's foot caught in the bear trap and severed except for one stringy tendon she snapped with a flick of her knife—puts extra pressure on the heart. My own physician had included "bad heart" on my medical record, which I took personally until he explained it was one of many risks I faced with my own pitiful leg.

"Keep moving," I agreed, impressed with her philosophical take on life. Plus, I didn't want to cross her. After all, to reach her heights, I had to kill two more men while standing on one foot. "Words to live by."

"No," she shook her head. "I mean, keep moving. This castle smells like a rotten egg with a dead chick inside. I need fresh air."

We climbed until we emerged on the roof, where Tip-Top gulped air as if she'd been drowning. In the distance on the Mississippi River, a two-tiered cake of a riverboat sparkled with frosty white lights. Its calliope piped shrilly. Between us and the river, the dauphine was seated on the rampart, his back to us. The wind teased the fringe of his cape. The fringe was leather, I think, but tipped in the same gold as the cape. I would give a million dollars for that cape. He absentmindedly kicked his legs against the wall. I imagined the turned-up toes of his shoes bobbing with each kick. The precariousness of his perch, the long fall to the jagged pavement—my unease thrummed into life.

"You said, 'you,'" I said to St. Claude, inching closer to him.

"Say again." The saint cupped a hand to his ear.

"You said, 'As you go forward.' Aren't you coming with?"

"I've equipped you with your familiars. Two extra, in fact." He made a lazy hand wave, as if sending me on my way.

All of my fake self-assurance evaporated. The man who had quickly become my most favorite saint in the whole world, who dressed exactly like I would if God ever let me be a saint, who gave me my own red jumpsuit, was leaving me. He was expecting me to be the leader of my freethinking grannies, for whom I had always been a happy lapdog.

I halted that runaway train of thoughts. I had set this story in motion. Complaining now would make me a terrible whiner who blamed others when they couldn't take care of their own little red wagon.

Chin held high, I asked, "Where are we going, me and my

grannies?"

He stared at the young man, who was wiping his mouth with one forearm then the other. "The dauphine will tell you. And you will tell him. As you so eloquently put it, you'll figure this shit out together."

"Don't be cute," I said but did not stop to wonder about the full implication of his comment. At the time, I merely made a mental note that my thoughts did not seem to be my own.

The riverboat calliope released its tune, "When the Saints Go Marching In."

I burst out laughing. "No way. My vision is set to that kitsch?"

Claude drew up, insulted. "Enough. Do your duty."

And with that he vanished, leaving me alone with my murderous grannies and the dauphine.

Chapter 12

The view from the castle roof was amazing. The river sludged by in the crescent that gave the city its nickname. An oil tanker ready to return to sea sat at the Poland Street Wharf. The tanker was massive, bigger than an office building, bigger than the decrepit naval station that would make a perfect setting for a horror movie if a rich director ever noticed it. Across the river on the West Bank, a steeple rose from a church in Algiers. Storybook, all of it. The tanker, the hulking ogre; the steeple, the willowy princess. On the rampart, a prince known as the dauphine.

"My beautiful city." He stretched his arms toward the vista. "What I wouldn't give to clasp her to my breast. To sweep my cape and protect her from all manner of devils who would use her for their own purposes, stripping her of her majestic—"

I cleared my throat.

The dauphine looked over his shoulder. Was he returned from the time when the French ruled New Orleans and the only legal religion was Catholicism? I didn't know, but he could have been a Botticelli angel with his flushed cheeks, finely flared nostrils, and full bow lips. He studied us, and I saw what he saw: the Cherokee trapper; the prim old maid, the faux Southern Belle, and me in my red jumpsuit.

"Lose the rest of your guild?" he asked, as if we were a traveling troupe of actors. "What might your play be? Something . . . comedic?"

I had been swirling into the vortex that opens when you meet someone so incredibly gorgeous you can only stare—twice in my twenty-eight years it had happened—but his quip snapped me out of it. Him in his white stockings and blue velvet knickers and diamond earring shaped like a cross dangling from his earlobe. Acting all superior when he could be Mick Jagger.

"St. Claude sent us," I said, determined not to stare at his long eyelashes.

The dauphine twisted on the rampart so his legs hung on our side. The ankles of his white stockings were embroidered with a fleur-de-lis like a long-tailed trident, a nineteenth-century flourish, as Bigmama would say. In his current position, he could hop onto the roof or, if he leaned back just a bit, splat onto the sidewalk.

"And why might Claude have picked you?" He pointed one by one, pausing to give each of us his full attention. Apparently, death didn't shield one from the power of sexual energy. My grannies shifted and shuffled. The effect was made more irritating by his not seeming to be aware of his beauty. Or maybe he was so used to stunning us poor females he took it for granted.

"Claude didn't pick us. I did this." I circled my hand in the air, indicating the whole damn thing, including him, which I couldn't bring myself to say out loud. His eyes were deep blue. They smoked. I began to regret my jumpsuit request.

My attraction to the dauphine mortified me. If what the saint had said was true, I was Narcissus mooning into the pool, though Lord help if anyone had ever called me gorgeous. My mouth was big—I'm talking Julia Roberts big—and so were my eyes, which were set too far toward the edge of my skull. I wore my hair straight and pushed it behind my ears. Folks stared at me, sure, but it was to figure out exactly what was wrong with my face. The only traits the dauphine and I shared in common were our navy blue eyes and black hair, except I had bleached mine gray and it was growing out, so it was kinda Lady Frankenstein.

Elfy had separated herself from the group. She stood beside the dauphine and laid her dainty palms on the rampart. She gazed at the magnificent view. Sighing, she drank it all in then hiked up her skirt, slung a leg over the rampart, and crowded on top of the wall next to the dauphine. She patted his knee. I momentarily feared she had switched sides, but maybe she was helping in her own way. Bigmama opened her journal and sketched the scene, squinting to take it in. But it felt like a diversion to me, a way to deal with her reaction to the young man. Even Tip-Top averted her eyes. Why the hell had the saint sent us a bombshell?

"What did Claude tell you? Did he say I refused to rule?" The dauphine looked to Elfy for confirmation, as if they both knew what a rapscallion the saint was.

"He did mention it, but that's not his main concern," I said as Elfy closed the gap between her and the dauphine. "He's worried about you."

"Did he tell you why I won't rule?"

"It's too hard?" I guessed because I couldn't remember exactly what the saint had said, but it was something like that. Bigmama swept charcoal lines across her journal page then displayed it to the dauphine, which earned her a high-wattage smile.

A squib of doubt wormed into my consciousness. If we were supposed to persuade the dauphine, I hadn't brought the best backup team. These women were less about talk and more about action, deception, manipulation, and in Tip-Top's case, swift resolution.

"Ask him why he doesn't want to rule," Tip-Top directed, startling me out of my thoughts.

My surprise made me hesitate, and the dauphine jumped in.

"I don't wish to die." He directed his response to me. Either he recognized me as the leader, or the exact opposite. The assertiveness of the others had thrown him, and he viewed me as more pliable. "Did Claude tell you that? If I rule, I die?"

"He did suggest danger was somehow involved." I searched for something inspirational to say in favor of doing one's duty but got nothing. In fact, how had I been sent to encourage anyone to conform to societal—or saintly—expectations? That couldn't be right.

"Okay," I said. "Let's look at it from a different angle." On the river, the fancy riverboat slowly pulled away from the dock, its paddlewheel churning. "Maybe it's okay to reject the life set for you. Maybe what Claude really wanted was for us to help you escape."

Ignoring the tinkling bell at the back of my brain—what exactly had running away accomplished for me?—I motioned to the group. "It's our specialty, escaping. We've got mad skills with scheming and concocting diversionary plots, and you know . . ." I trailed off—he didn't need to know everything about my grannies. "We can make it happen if you'll get off the rampart."

"Rather than your empty promises, why don't you actually help me?"

"Help you how?" I said, frustration creeping into my voice.

Elfy slipped her arm around the prince's waist. He gently removed it and looked me in the eye, all pretense gone. This dauphine—stark appraisal, intelligent assessment—was way more dangerous than the white-legginged one.

"Help me find the person who wants me dead."

Chapter 13

I'm really sorry, but before I disclose who wanted the dauphine dead, I need you to bear with one more interruption. (I'll be quick, I promise.)

You have to understand how my ancestors died.

Earlier, I mentioned these three women died on the same day. From that, you might conclude they knew each other. They did not. They lived at the same time in the same state but in different worlds. Tip-Top limped around her makeshift post office in the hardscrabble Piney Woods, proud of successfully raising her son into adulthood, proud of not succumbing entirely to the redneck culture she'd married into. Elfy polished her silver demitasse spoons and fluffed her needlepointed pillows in Jackson, her sons the lords of society, her daughters sought-after prizes. Bigmama wrote her odes to the Confederacy in the river town of Vicksburg where she was published so often in the Warren County paper she was named an honorary member of the Magnolia Press Coalition and given an enameled pin she never removed from the collar of her dour dresses. Strangers until the day they died, together.

Here's what happened. According to my own grannies, y'all.

In 1873, following the disaster of the Civil War, beleaguered Mississippi needed a breather from the cruel violence aimed at ending Reconstruction. The reason to celebrate had to be a safe bet. No, not kids with cancer, that hadn't started yet. Back then, the safe bet was mothers. Who could complain about an ode to mothers, even if the particular mothers to be honored weren't the African American women who had managed to keep their children alive during decades of economic exploitation and white oppressor slaughter. Nope. Mississippi would honor those who had birthed the soldiers who wore Confederate gray and fought to keep the African American mothers enslaved.

Anywho.

The Mississippi Motherhood Celebration was the brainchild of the president pro tem of the state senate, a portly man from Jackson, and as Elfy said of her ancestor's son, the most powerful politician in the state. The president pro tem formed a committee composed of his cronies. The committee chose a famous female author from Warren County to pen the ode to the mothers. They secured use of the Vicksburg courthouse for the ceremony—classy, plus it would redeem the humiliation of Pemberton's surrender to Grant at that very courthouse (redemption was big in Mississippi at the time). The front steps, being the actual site of surrender, were considered tainted, but fortunately the courthouse was double-sided. The back had an almost identical columned facade. The reading of the commissioned ode would take place on those steps. To curry favor, the committee asked the dainty mother of the president pro tem to stand on stage as the physical embodiment of ideal motherhood. Not to be outdone, the committee chair invited his more rustic ma to attend too. Or, as Tippy put it, "to be their Indian."

The week of the event, the Motherhood Committee traveled to Vicksburg to approve preparations and drink brown liquor—

the committee was a choice appointment. To get the biggest bang for the buck, the committee set the ceremony the day before statewide elections. They hammered up a podium and swagged it with bunting. In a flash of brilliance, they hired the bawdy musicians at the Bluff River Tavern to "fill the courthouse lawn with delight," according to the newspaper article my Bigmama smoothed with her palm and read to me. The committee's work done, the hungover men returned to their hometowns. Only the committee chair stayed for the ceremony, because his rustic ma asked him to.

As usual in Mississippi, everything got f'd up. Warren County (and just about every other county in the state) had decided the days of Black Republican voting were over. The Warren County Red Shirts tapped junior member Jeremy Monger to set off a small charge on Election Day to frighten the ne'er-do-wells streaming to the courthouse to vote. Once the scalawags and Republicans had scattered, the Whites would descend and cast their ballots.

Monger had perfected his explosive art during the war. A banty rooster of a man, he was confident in his ability to set the charge beneath the courthouse steps and leave the building unscathed. "All I can say, musta tooken a mighty talented man to lay that charge so's not a scratch was left on the courthouse," the article quoted him as saying afterward.

Monger was also conscientious. Unwilling to wait until the morning of the election and aware of the ceremony the day prior, he laid down the gunpowder charge two days before the election. That hot morning he crawled under the dark steps.

At this point in Bigmama's telling, I would lean in. Her eyes glittered. "Flat on his belly, Monger inched his flabby white body across the dirt. Sweat stung his eyes. As his stubby fingers twisted the charge, he dreamed of glory. He would be the hero who saved the election. An unsung hero, which made it that much sweeter." When I asked what became of him, the man who had murdered my grannies, Bigmama said, "According to my Bigmama, Monger was the one who, still trying to prove himself a decade later, fired on the Carroll County Courthouse, setting off the Carrollton Massacre where he got knifed in the brain."

I found an entry on the Carroll County killings in the Encyclopedia Britannica that said the courthouse ambush of Black folks with the temerity to take White folks to court had started over spilled molasses. When I showed the page to Bigmama, she shrugged. "That's what I said. The man was a maggot."

The afternoon of the Motherhood Ceremony, the Stars and Bars flapped in the river breeze. Various city officeholders and dignitaries lined up behind the three women standing in the front. The committee chair uncharacteristically joined the dignitaries, proud of his willingness to give the women a moment in the sun.

The author, who we know as Bigmama, was out front at the podium, standing tall in her black ankle-length dress. She wore a no-nonsense grimace. ("Though her entire professional career had been devoted to writing nonsense," Elfy would throw in as she stirred the pot at the stove.) To the author's left, the president pro tem's mother did him proud. ("In her silly Southern getup with a straw hat and frilly parasol," Bigmama retorted, glaring at Elfy.) Only the Piney Woods ma, a.k.a. Tip-Top, looked ill at ease, her senses on high alert at this fabricated ceremony that invited comeuppance.

Tip-Top never had the chance to sling her bowie knife. Elfy's pearl-handled pistol stayed hidden in the folds of her hoop skirt. Bigmama, busy reading her speech, left un-brandished the leather cudgel she always carried on her belted sash. There was no warning when a horse tethered at the step's railing pranced sideways, its shoe throwing a spark. No time to react when the spark lit an oddly placed string running from beneath the steps. No moment of understanding before the running flame ate up the fuse to the carefully laid gunpowder.

"The women never knew what hit 'em," Bigmama said. The lone man in the back survived.

"Isn't that always the case?" sighed Elfy.

The deaths don't much make the history books. In the *Vicksburg Gazette* article quoting Monger, they included before and after sketches of the courthouse steps. One of the audience members said, "It's a crying shame, the damage done to those great courthouse steps."

You see why my grannies were skittish around each other. Boom! You'd be skittish too. I'm sure the sight of each other did not spark happy memories.

So, if and when my grannies don't live up to your expectations of a heroic trio, don't blame them. Blame the committee that wanted to use women for propaganda. Blame maggoty Jeremy Monger. Blame the horse that shied. Blame everything that goes into the soup that becomes who we are, but whatever you do, when my ancestors, who were brought forth only to help in my quest totally mess it up, don't blame them. Or me. In this only, I am blameless.

Chapter 14

When last we saw him, the dauphine was declaring someone wanted him dead. What a stroke of luck, I told him, as me and my krewe were experts on murder. (I saw no reason to specify we were experts on committing the act.) He visibly brightened, and we all left the rampart together.

I lugged open the castle's heavy front door and breathed deeply. Summer heat in New Orleans was metallic, dangerous in its jagged edges. Now in October, the heat was clear as glass. No humidity, and the scents lacing the air less noisy. Geraniums in second bloom, okra in the side yard, life was restored. The soggy became neat, the stinky fresh, a time when all of us—man, woman, and babbling child—believed the Saints would go all the way this year. New Orleans owned the fall, and my ragtag group owned New Orleans.

As we streamed onto the street, my heart swelled with pride. We would do this thing. We would thwart whoever was threatening the dauphine. I would save a life as randomly as I'd been forced to take one, and my amazing posse of criminally inclined grannies would help. For once, the universe would set aside its weighted scales of justice and let the women win.

I loped after the group, which was quickly disappearing around the corner as they scampered away from St. Claude, the street, not the saint who really was gone.

I gained on them very gradually. You'd think Tip-Top's gimpy foot would slow them down, but apparently she made better time with her infirmity than I did with mine.

"Hey, guys—wait up!" I called.

"Cain't," Elfy threw back at me, her gaze ahead. "That's the one, in the black lace gown. She's getting away."

Part III

The Pursuit

Chapter 15

The figure we pursued melted into a pop-up store on Burgundy Street. Its snub nose door sat diagonally on the corner lot. The site was always taking on one personality or another. The last time I'd been in, a leftover hippie couple had been hawking those oversized Easter eggs with chickens and ducks frolicking inside. Except in these eggs, the ducks were doing things they shouldn't have been doing to the chickens. Now, cheap plastic skulls swayed from the house eaves. The Bywater was truly going to shit.

We crowded into the front room, close. We smelled. Musty old velvet and thick heavy wool and tanned animal skins. And from Elfy, the scent that made you stop on the sidewalk and search for its source until you spied the narcissus nodding in the spring breeze: a delicate coming-and-going scent. Paperwhites, my Elfy called them. At Christmastime, the interior of the pie safe was humid with pea gravel-filled bowls closeted in the dark to force blooming. Here in New Orleans, Elfy herself was the white-cupped bloom; her past, the generative darkness.

I pushed her toward the front of the group. At least the clerk wouldn't hold his nose.

"Ask him where the redhead in black lace went," I whispered as Elfy's black booties slid across the polished wood floor.

The clerk leaned on the glass countertop, twirling a strand of hair in his fingers. He wore a plaid cape that was really a long coat whose arms had been repositioned to tie the cape. His nails were sparkly yellow. Late forties maybe, he seemed like someone who had finally decided to be himself. He blinked his mascaraed lashes at Elfy. She blinked back, and for a moment I thought they were going to engage in an eyelash battle. Elfy would've won, lashes down.

Instead, she palmed the clerk's jawline and swiveled his head left and right. "You have the most perfect cheekbones," she said with a sigh and released his jaw. "Are your ankles as exquisite?"

He motioned for her to come around the counter. The shop featured vintage clothes repurposed into Halloween costumes, but the counter's glass shelves held overly-iced cookies featuring ghosts and bats doing naughty things, making me wonder if the pop-up insisted each tenant provide at least a bit of sugared pornography.

Positioning herself where the clerk indicated, Elfy examined his stuck out leg then, lifting the hem of her skirt, laid her ankle against his. Heads angled, they studied their delicate bones. I was mesmerized by Elfy's intuitive seduction. How did she know this skeletal approach would appeal? My own Elfy had been way past her flirting days, all her energy funneled into dusting and cleaning . . . and fingering mushroom-topped objects.

"I'm Elfy," the first Elfy cooed, swiveling her ankle this way and that. In return, the clerk warbled, "Wally," the two of them regular love-birds. Tip-Top and Bigmama looked on, their faces drawn up like they were sucking on unripe persimmons.

Offended by Elfy's methods, no doubt. Tip-Top clicked her cheek in disapproval, but Bigmama ignored her, as if she no more wanted to align herself with Tip-Top than she did with Elfy. Reaching to the small of her back, she removed her journal where it was tucked in her thick grosgrain sash and began writing. Her leather cudgel swayed on the sash, and I expected her words—as usual—were as full of finesse as the heavy cudgel.

"A woman we were following came in here. A redhead wearing black lace. She looked . . . big-boned." Elfy searched the clerk's face. "Did I imagine that?"

"No, love. She's built like a Rock 'Em Sock 'Em Robot. Thick-bodied, but glides when she walks. She's been here all morning with her gaggle of red-caped minions. So *Handmaid's Tale*." Wally adjusted his own handmade cape. "Grande Red, I call her. She tells those women to have at someone, they start pecking. I came close to throwing the lot of them out. They were all over a poor covey of bridesmaids. Fuming to her hussies about some guy defying her and taking it out on a bunch of drunk ladies wearing tiaras."

Wally stared at the dauphine, who slumped against a plaster statue of a spinal column. "You the one Grande Red's mad at?"

"She's a terrible woman who's vowed to harm this poor defenseless dauphine for no good reason," I huffed to the clerk. My initial thrill that the dauphine had an enemy was blossoming into active dislike of said enemy. Picking on drunken bachelorettes, the greatest ambassadors the city had ever known. Who did this Grande Red think she was? She was a bully, that's what. The type who gathered sycophants and used them as arrows to sling at other women. I bet those bridesmaids weren't paying her one ounce of attention, which was probably what made her mad. "If we don't stop her, she's gonna kill him when he takes the throne," I added.

"The throne, you say?" Wally continued to address the dauphine, who was looking more and more uncomfortable. "She told her minions you've grown impossible. What'd you do to piss her off?"

"I don't know her," the dauphine declared. "Never seen her before in my life. Have no idea who she is."

His thrice denial made me believe, like lying Peter throwing Jesus under the bus, he knew her all too well.

Chapter 16

"What the hell?" I demanded, my anger flaring. Here I was trying to protect the dauphine, and he was lying about his relationship with his nemesis, keeping secrets . . . being exactly like the me he was.

I drew a calming breath—this trying to get along with myself was going to be harder than I thought. "Okay, spill it. Who is she?"

The dauphine rolled his eyes. "She's a retrograde who can't look to the future, and instead of confronting me directly, sneaks around to stab me in the back. Literally. Isn't that enough?"

"No," I said since he'd given me the option. "Why does she want to murder you?"

"No one said murder."

"You did."

"I didn't."

"You did. You said someone wanted you dead."

"Dead does not equal murder."

"Oh, right," I said. He had a point, one around which most of my life revolved. "Who wants to kill you?"

He picked up a Humpty-Dumpty doll in red-striped leggings and casually tossed it from hand to hand. "I may have misspoke. She doesn't want to kill me *per se*. But she does want me to take action that will leave me dead." He dropped the doll, and it bounced under the counter. "She is a traitor to the crown, the worst type. One who cannot distinguish between her selfish desires and the good of her country."

There was so much more I wanted to ask. Who exactly was she? What future did she reject? What did she want him to do that was so lethal? And if she was a weaselly female who bullied other women, was she from Mississippi?

But I held my tongue and focused on the question at hand. "Where did Grande Red go?" I asked Wally the clerk, as she obviously wasn't in the room.

Wally produced a toothpick, popped it in his mouth, and shifted it from side to side, considering.

"Now, if she was a customer, I wouldn't tell you a thing. I don't run down customers, no matter how rude. But has she bought one item, spent one dime? No. She just causes trouble with the real customers. 'She's shopping,' her minions say. Shopping my ass. She was spying, sorting out her next move. I bet she lured y'all here. And I don't mean to be ugly, but this group . . ." His gaze hovered over me and the three grannies. "If you're chasing a pissed off Grande Red, you'll need reinforcements. Y'all got your hands full with him."

The dauphine, palm pressed to the wall, was leaning over a potted palm. Heaving, he vomited pink bile into its thick yellow roots.

"Excuse me." Wally swung past Elfy, and lifting the palm, carted it swaying toward the door. At the threshold he stopped, swirling his cape. His gaze had hardened. We had violated the one true rule of native New Orleanians: Don't throw up in the potted palm. He nodded at the curtain against the back wall.

"Grande Red went in there." Softening, he winked at Elfy. "Come back when you got more time, love. Get you out of that dotted swiss, you'd be something."

He stepped outside.

The dauphine raked his forearm across his mouth, a gesture I recognized from earlier. In truth, he didn't seem drunk, but he did have the sheepish look of one sobering up. The sour smell of vomit had not departed with the palm.

"You up for this?" I asked. His alabaster skin had turned pea green.

"A little vertigo, is all." He tried to smile, but his eyes were jumping like a gigged frog. "Sobering up is making me feel quite odd. Maybe I was meant to stay drunk on my rampart."

Now, that confused me. I hadn't wanted him to stay on the rampart. It was my idea we leave the castle to find the one who wanted to kill him, so who was this person who meant him to stay there drunk? Was I or was I not in charge of my own vision?

He added, "No matter. Perhaps I can suffocate her with the stink of vomit."

Bigmama, her pen scratching notes in her journal, snickered.

"Come on," I said, and held the back curtain open for the others to file through. Ready to duck in myself, I heard the front door squeak open.

Wally popped his head in.

"Be careful." He grinned maliciously. "She's armed."

Chapter 17

The back room of the pop-up store hadn't gotten the word about the twenty-first century. The lamps were gas, the floor dirt. Brick braces held up crude wooden shelves. The shelves were piled with boned bodices and other satiny costumes—inventory, I decided. But also seashells and paintings of the Madonna and an entire shelf of red beans. When I saw the bunnies and chicks from the Easter pop-up, I decided prior tenants had left bits of themselves behind.

My hand on my sword hilt, I did a quick assessment of the space, hunting for a place Grande Red could hide. She wasn't hiding. She had escaped. On the far wall, a Dutch door stood ajar. The orange leaves of a crepe myrtle waved through the door's open upper half.

I lunged at the doorknob, but Tip-Top threw out her arm, stopping me.

"It's not real," she said, and I saw what she meant. The door was painted on, one of those trick-of-the-eye 3D murals New Orleans loved.

"Trompe l'oeil," Bigmama said, running her fingers across the mural. "Our parlor had one, birds of paradise swinging in a gilded cage. Baby Jewel would crawl toward the bright flowers, saying, 'Bird! Bird!'" Pivoting, Bigmama glanced around the room. "They're meant to distract. Ours took greedy eyes away from the silver goblets in the china cabinet. There."

She pointed to a full-length mirror angled to reflect the blazing crepe myrtle and Dutch door. Beside the mirror, a party machine belched fog.

"Someone's idea of a joke," the dauphine said, gripping the mirror on both sides and lifting. "A smoke screen. Telling us the way out is behind the mirror."

Bigmama wrinkled her nose in distaste as the dauphine worked the heavy mirror off its hook. Maybe it was his white leggings or the fuchsia ribbon tying his black curls. Or maybe she found the strands of vomit on the curls disgusting. Anyway, whatever initial attraction she'd had to him had evaporated. So be it, but he was our ward. We were protecting him from a ruthless enemy. And I suspected he was dealing with things we didn't quite understand. His queasy stomach didn't seem to be entirely from drink.

As the dauphine set the cumbersome mirror on the floor, he fumed. "'Grande Red,' my lord. That's glorifying her, that's what that is. Last thing she needs is glorifying. She can do that all on her own, thank you very much."

"What's she to you?" I asked, helping him walk the mirror down the wall. From what I'd glimpsed, she was too old to be a girlfriend, but not really old. She'd run swiftly, if heavily, like a linebacker who intercepts the ball and lumbers toward the goal line.

Misjudging the distance, I walked the heavy gold mirror onto the dauphine's toe.

With a yelp, he jumped aside, wincing. At my apology, he held up a palm. "It was an accident. Forgive my outburst."

He was more gracious than I would have been, someone

dropped a heavy mirror on my toe. I'd be hopping in circles, holding my foot and cursing. Could he possibly be the better part of me? That idea—a member of the ego-driven, condescending, violent opposite sex could represent my better self—was hard for me to swallow.

The dauphine re-attacked the mirror, his profile earnest. Surely he understood the logistics of it. If there were a door behind the mirror, it would lead back into the front room. Yet, I was reluctant to interrupt his efforts, protecting his—my?—hope in spite of physical reality.

But when he finally shoved the mirror aside, I'd be danged if a door didn't appear.

"Aha!" he exclaimed and grabbed the doorknob. The door didn't give. Bracing his slippered foot against the wall, he wrenched open the stubborn door. Dankness whooshed out. We both peered inside. His vomit smell was gone, replaced by something similar to licorice. The puff of his breath was delicate against my ear and tickled. I swatted it away.

We were staring at a hallway. To the left, another door opened, and I realized the pop-up was an old side-by-side converted to a single. The dauphine and I leaned in, the group huddled behind us. At the end of the hallway, the flame of an iron sconce flickered. It illuminated a flight of steep stairs, their treads eroded by time. Together, the group edged toward the steps like one giant millipede. At the foot of the staircase, a tunnel curved out of sight toward the river.

The hallway made a ticking noise like a furnace in winter. A seeping gas smell wafted up from the tunnel, plus mildew and something stinky—not the dauphine. Something I recognized.

"Dead squirrel," Bigmama said.

"The expired one," I confirmed, because that's what the exterminator in his white jumpsuit called the squirrels that regularly died behind Elfy's flowered wallpaper. Drilling a tiny hole in the plaster, he would carefully draw out a carcass, flat as a ballet slipper, and display it on his palm for me to examine.

Dead, that which had so recently been scrabbling through the walls, nails clicking on the wooden studs. Now awaiting burial in Bigmama's garden, service conducted by preacher me. The comforting death smell of the tunnel gave me hope. We had found where the rot lay.

"Grande Red made this tunnel," Bigmama said, examining its rough-hewn nature. "It's her creation, and the author is always in charge of her creations. We enter at our peril."

That didn't sound right. Surely Grande Red had arrived in modern day New Orleans at the same time as the dauphine, which meant she'd been in the city for a handful of hours. Long enough to scout out the pop-up and harass its customers, but she couldn't have excavated the smelly tunnel. She sure could have slunk down it.

"I'll go first, then y'all—" I began.

Later, I wondered if Elfy's intuitive sense of the ego of men had warned her to clamp onto the dauphine's arm, and the dauphine, feeling her restraint, rebelled. At the time, I thought she was flirting with him, and he, a typical male, hadn't listened to what I said.

He stepped onto the stairs.

With a screech the step retracted beneath his feet, and arms flailing, he disappeared into the dark.

Chapter 18

The hallway was quiet after the dauphine's departure. Elfy sniffled, and Bigmama cleared her throat. Tip-Top laid her palm on my shoulder, turning me to face her.

"We have lost the one we chased and also the one we were to protect."

It was a big speech for Tip-Top, who was much more self-contained than my Tippy. I could not see her boiling salty peanuts for my snack or fighting me for the covers in her bed. But then Tip-Top smoothed my hair, cupping her palms to my skull, and I slowly shut my eyes. All three of my grannies had done that. Not because my hair was fly-away or messy. It was sleek as an otter, begging to be touched.

Tip-Top's palm was calloused, bumpy, and rough. The family story was that she refused to do women's work in the house and went into the fields to chop cotton with the men. When she tired of that, she showed up at the post office and claimed the right to sort mail, which is where she lost her foot in the bear trap (which somehow also involved a possum). Early on, I concluded someone didn't want her in the post office and set the trap for her to walk into—wasn't like a bear was gonna steal the mail.

The trap that took my own foot was tuberculosis. Not of the lungs, of the hip. When my limp got so pronounced my parents finally sent me to a specialist, antibiotics cleared it up, but the hip was irreversibly damaged. With the blood supply cut off, my calf had withered. I'm convinced the hiring team at the ad agency knew about the injury. The drama club at the community college had held a big-ass rally to raise money for a new experimental (and failed) surgery to restore blood flow to the lower leg. The firm probably heard about the fundraiser, and rolled my infirmity into my affirmative action score. I know my future boss was aware. He walked in on me one time when I was adjusting the brace that steadied my leg. Later he went after me like a lion sighting a wounded gazelle.

I felt myself leaning into Tip-Top's palm, suddenly overwhelmed by my failure to hold onto the dauphine.

"I failed before we even got good and started." Aware of my pitiful tone, I warned myself not to revert to childhood behavior just because I was with my faux grannies.

"Nonsense. A mere setback is all." Bigmama eyed Tip-Top, who was positioning me at the head of the staircase. The dark stairs where the dauphine had disappeared wavered under the flickering light from the sconce.

"Listen carefully, child," she said, exactly like my Tippy.

After she was sure she had my attention, Tip-Top stepped on the threshold. But rather than walking forward, she hopped to the right. The first step quickly retracted, gliding out of sight. Anyone proceeding onto the step, such as the dauphine, would have fallen into the hole that now gaped. When Tip-Top gingerly stepped back onto the threshold, the step reappeared.

"A pressure plate," Tip-Top said. "Like a jackknife." She knelt and, without removing her weight from the threshold, smoothed her palm across the magic step. It wasn't pocked like the others.

"It's never been used," I said. "How'd you know?"

"Listen. You must listen."

This time when Tip-Top stepped to the side, I heard a slight swish.

"I'll be damned," I breathed.

"There is always a mechanical explanation," said my granny who died over a hundred and fifty years before. "Look, listen, figure out how it works."

She led me back to the storage room, grabbed a Hello Kitty backpack from a shelf, and shoved it at me. "Carry this. You, too," she said to the others who had followed us. "Find something useful, then we depart."

When we were all provisioned, Tip-Top selected a flambeau leaning beside the faux Dutch door, and we reentered the hallway. She tilted the flambeau—the torch that led off the nighttime Mardi Gras parades, the carriers twirling their flambeaux, fire jumping off the reflective metal sheets, orange magic squirming into the night—to the sconce flame.

The flambeau's wadded cotton ignited.

"Go." Tip-Top waved me toward the staircase. "Don't step on the trickster step."

Chapter 19

My murderous grannies and I descended the stairs, gripping its satiny railing, until the staircase that was still part of a house ended abruptly at the rocky tunnel. Tip-Top held up a palm for us to halt and, head swiveling, examined her surroundings.

We waited. Water dripped, echoing through the tunnel.

Satisfied, Tip-Top motioned us forward, but not into the tunnel. She led us around the staircase to a small door in the slope of the stairs.

The room under the staircase. The place in every story where all the bad things lurked. The door was ajar, the heavy beam that should have barred it, unhinged. I drew my sword, ready. Bigmama acted first, poking her head inside.

"Gone," she said. She craned her neck to examine the trap door in the ceiling where the startled dauphine would have whooshed into what was essentially a cage. The space was too sloped for all of us to fit in comfortably. We parted so Tip-Top and her flambeau could examine it.

"Not gone. Shrunk." Tip-Top angled the flambeau to light a dark corner of the room. A baby sat cross-legged on the floor. The baby's navy blue eyes followed us as we crowded into the room, stooping be damned.

"Is that the dauphine?" I re-sheathed my sword, embarrassed to have drawn on a baby. He had the dauphine's eyes and black curls. But he wasn't shrunk. "Look at his clothes," I said. His little boy suit—maroon brocade jacket, black satin britches with diamond stitching up the side—wasn't the dauphine's. Same style, but no stockings or fringed cape or shoes with turned-up toes. Whatever he was, the child was barefoot and happy, giggling and spitting bubbles.

Tip-Top lifted the blanket the child sat on. Not a blanket, a gold-trimmed cape. Last we'd seen it, the cape had been teetering with the dauphine on the trick step. "You are right. The dauphine, our dauphine was here. Now he's gone with this one left in his place," Tip-Top said.

"That one won't do us any good." Bigmama turned to leave, but Elfy shoved Tip-Top aside and, quick as a minute, scooped up the changeling. The boy, who didn't look old enough to walk, patted her face with dimpled fingers, and I imagined the baby Delores Elfy had lost.

"I want him," Elfy declared.

A baby on a quest was a weird thing, but despite my family's fraught history with babies, I was willing to keep my mouth shut given Elfy's loss and all. Apparently, Bigmama was not.

"He's not yours to take."

"But he was given to us." Elfy clasped the baby to her breast.

Bigmama scowled at Elfy. This Bigmama couldn't know about Elfy's dead child, and like my own Bigmama, compassion did not appear to be her default setting.

"Grande Red took the dauphine and left that decoy so we'd go, 'Ga, ga, a baby.'" Bigmama threw up her hands. "She's tricking us into abandoning the chase, and you're falling for it."

"You can't seriously suggest we leave this child

unattended?" Elfy shielded the boy as if Bigmama meant him harm.

"We have no business with that child. Our job is to get the dauphine to assume the throne"—Bigmama caught my look—"or help him live the life he wants. We need the adult dauphine, not a baby."

"We can do both. We can hunt down Grande Red and keep the baby." Elfy jiggled the child and offered him a wide-eyed look of surprise, which he returned. "If you aren't ready to deal with whatever this quest brings, you should turn back."

While they argued, I looked to Tip-Top for help, but she shrugged her shoulders in a "you decide" gesture. I realized she expected me to break the tie between Bigmama and Elfy.

Did the baby stay? Or did the baby come with us?

—

I couldn't choose between Bigmama and Elfy, never could. Not on the mornings when Bigmama took extra time with her letters making us late for our walks in the garden so reminiscent of her time in the prison yard. When that happened, as Bigmama and I circled, Elfy stood at the kitchen door, squinting through the screen. I could feel her mournful impatience as we circled and circled. Elfy wouldn't start her cleaning without me, and Bigmama wouldn't be hurried. The tension between the two turned my hands clammy. Bigmama would unclasp my hand, wipe her palm against her skirt, and slip her hand back in mine.

We kept walking.

By the time she released me, my entire shirt would be drenched with sweat and my sneakers squeaked. Later in life I would never be able to hear the words *flop sweat* without feeling again Bigmama's palm slicking mine, the squish of my Keds against my instep.

I ended the torture by rising early one morning and sneaking Bigmama's notebook from her kitchen drawer. Flipping the pages, I struck through the next three names on her running list of letters to be written. It worked. She didn't notice she had not, in fact, written those letters, and her session went quickly enough to accommodate Elfy's longing. I repeated my trick until I reached the summer of my ninth grade when Elfy died in her sleep, Bigmama suffered a terminal stroke, and I was left with only Tippy to love me. My parents kept sending me to the Jackson mansion for my summers as if nothing had happened—"You're old enough to drive, you're old enough to stay by yourself." I walked the garden alone each morning, dusted and polished alone each afternoon. Altering Bigmama's list was my first act of petty vandalism, but like all that followed, I claimed self-defense.

—

As I watched Elfy make funny faces at the baby, I wished St. Claude was here for guidance. I hadn't thought to ask him what to do if we found a baby along the way. In all honesty, St. Claude could have done a better prep job, offering a bit more insight into what was coming.

But he had, hadn't he?

Way back at the beginning when I asked why he thought I would be sympathetic to the spoiled-brat heir to the throne, Claude corrected me, saying I might want to see the dauphine die. I didn't want to see anyone die. I'd had way too much of that in my life already. I particularly didn't want my doppelgänger to die. Surely I couldn't be that self-destructive? One thing for sure, whether the kid was the dauphine made young, a decoy, or a random baby, I would never want the cutie pie, roly-poly child to buy it. If we took him with us, there was no way I could harbor a secret wish for his grown-up self to die. Perhaps that attachment would shield the dauphine from the specter of violent death that loped behind me like a starving dog.

"He's good luck," I said to Elfy, avoiding Bigmama's eye. "Keep him."

Elfy beamed at me while Bigmama sputtered, but before she

could get anything out, Tip-Top handed her the flambeau and relieved me of the Hello Kitty backpack. She stuffed the baby in its mouth, secured it around Elfy's neck. "You fight amongst yourselves when you should be solving the problem: How can we take the baby and free our hands for defense?"

Elfy palmed the bottom of the baby's backpack. "So where is the dauphine?"

"In your backpack," I said.

"I meant the adult dauphine of course," she answered. "Not him as a baby."

Two dauphines? That hadn't been one of my options, but leave it to Elfy to see the essence of a man, even a tiny one.

"We're being led around by the nose," Bigmama said as we all snaked back into the tunnel.

"Perhaps we should not so readily follow." Elfy stared into the dark tunnel, absentmindedly stroking the baby's head. Wouldn't surprise me if she'd be perfectly happy to take the baby as a consolation prize and forget about the adult dauphine. But that, as my own Elfy would say, would not do.

"Right," I said, more curt than I intended. "We don't have a choice. Let's go."

I ducked into the little room, grabbed the dauphine's cape from the floor, and tied it around my neck. If Elfy could claim a baby, I could claim a kick-ass cape.

I led us off, and with little conversation we proceeded single file down the tunnel.

Chapter 20

The air in the tunnel was hot, close, and thick with the smell of chalk, thanks to the chunks that had fallen from the walls and gathered at our feet. When I tapped one with my sword, it mushed. Tip-Top passed me to take the lead. The flambeau cast weird shadows down the tunnel. I sweated in my jumpsuit. Tip-Top's foot dragged.

When I was ten years old, the doctors sent me to the hospital for the surgery that would cut my Achilles tendon to keep my foot from dropping. Bigmama sat by my bedside the entire time. She never released my hand. She told me about setting out the tomato plants too early (it wasn't yet April 15th) and that year's design for the pink and white caladiums. She described a trap she had laid for the squirrels and how hard it had been to scrub the hairy moss from the birdbath. As I meandered in and out of consciousness, she took me to our garden so completely I awoke and smelled sweet olive blooming in the sterile room.

When I came home from the hospital, Elfy took over with

spoonfuls of warm soup and kisses on my forehead to ward off fever. And when I had gained enough strength, she passed me off to Tippy who taught me how to operate the metal contraptions of the brace, so similar to the bit and bridle of a horse. I clicked it in place and grinned with pride. What good were two normal legs when you could have a special leg like my pioneer great-great-grandma Tip-Top? Not even the jeers of the hateful bastards in my fifth grade class—little Stalin-ettes with their chubby man boobs and Bugs Bunny teeth—could wipe the sheen off my contentment. I was bionic. I was badass.

If only I could have held onto that confidence. Instead, I too often overcompensated and blindly did the opposite of whatever was expected. Maybe that was my current problem. I was wedging myself into a reverse hero's journey where the damsel-not-in-distress rescued the handsome prince. My directional dyslexia might be coming into play, too, pointing us wrongly down this low-roofed, pickax-hewn tunnel to nowhere. Elfy might be the smart one. We should've taken the baby and run.

"We like to think the best of ourselves, but it's usually the opposite," Bigmama said, and I wondered if I had voiced my thoughts out loud. The hem of her dress brushed the ground as if in a procession. Behind us, Elfy kept up a line of jabber with the baby, who jabbered back. They had already developed their own language. In front, Tip-Top listened to Bigmama with one ear.

"That's what I learned when I was cowering in the cave with the ship bombardments shaking the ground. The only thing that kept me from running screaming into the line of fire wasn't courage or trust in God or devotion to country. It was the beautiful rocker I sat in. The family silver in the rosewood chest. The Mallard bed I lay awake in night after night. My fine things proved I was somebody. Fate would not render my life so stupidly meaningless as to die in that misbegotten war." She walked her fingers down the stone, and I wondered if her eyesight was poor—she was always touching her surroundings as if to orient herself. "I didn't place my faith in God. I placed it in a set of Limoges teacups."

"You spent the war with teacups?" Tip-Top asked. She shrugged out of her jacket one arm at a time, shifting the flambeau to her left hand while she did so, and laid the jacket over her arm. Her shoulders shuddered with her heavy breathing. Under her cotton shirt, a pad of fat rolled across her back.

"We were under siege. The women and children went into the breast of Mother Earth to protect ourselves," Bigmama explained. She pressed her palms against the small of her back, as if arching against a pain. No. Her fingers searched for and found the hard cover of the journal tucked in the backside of her sash. She patted it, comforting herself that it was still there.

"I spent the war with my backside against the cast iron stove, a shotgun pointed at the door." Tip-Top's voice came to us from where the tunnel curved to the left. "But when I needed it most, the gun hung up on me. I had to knife the man in the gut. My baby crawled through the man's congealing stomach slime." At the curve, Tip-Top waited for us, holding the flambeau butt-to-the-ground like a long rifle. "While you were hiding in a cave with a bed with its own name."

"Don't judge the ease of my time in the cave," Bigmama said, fury in her words.

"Hunh," Tip-Top grunted.

After a moment, Bigmama said in a more normal tone of voice, "I always told my Jewel she was conceived in that bed." A drop fell from the tunnel roof and hit her forehead. She wiped it off. "Never told her I was cowering in a cave."

Tip-Top cracked a smile. "I never told my Benjamin the man I killed was a river rat, not the Union soldier he imagined."

"And so the myth begins," Elfy said.

A concrete wall stopped us in our tracks. Moisture wept from its face. The dripping water smelled like leaves decaying in a puddle or the brown well water that filled Tippy's bathtub. Or the Mississippi River.

"We're in a smugglers' tunnel." I imagined pirates unloading untaxed goods from river pirogues and hauling the contraband into the Bywater.

I spun, cape twirling, to examine the mysterious tunnel we had traversed. The tunnel roof was reinforced with corrugated tin. Creosoted railroad ties propped up the junctures at the curve. "The trickster step was to protect the smugglers from anyone who might be pursuing them."

"Grande Red," Bigmama pronounced, satisfaction in her voice.

Again, I doubted it. Tunnels were rare in a city with such a low water table, but one did run underneath Canal Street. Maybe, while I was telling y'all the story of my grannies, Grande Red scouted around and found a way to smuggle the captured dauphine to the river and onto a ship to France. But the flood wall cut her off. In my mind I saw the top of the flood wall rising outside my apartment. How could I be in such a strange underground place but so near the rooms where I spent my normal days?

When I turned around, Tip-Top was pulling a ladder from the ceiling, a rickety thing like an attic ladder in a tract house. Its jointed sections creaked into place, and up Tip-Top went, pushing open the trap door. When she released sunlight into our eyes, Bigmama snuffed the flambeau and leaned the dead torch against the wall.

"You're gonna be outside my apartment." I grabbed a rung and climbed, my sword clanging against the metal. "This is my neighborhood. We could've walked down Montegut Street and arrived at the same damn spot. Quicker too."

But we must have taken a bigger segue than I thought because we emerged a good ways downriver from my apartment. The pedestrian bridge at Crescent Park arced to my left, its rusted steel flaking like a vampire hit by the sun. The bridge connected Chartres Street to the walking path that meandered beside the river. Locals strolled down the path in the descending dusk. A dude spun to untangle the leashes of two Dalmatians he was leading, while an oblivious old lady in headphones conducted music with sweeping arms. A damn army helicopter banked overhead, and even though I heard them all day every day, I wondered irrationally if it were St. Claude urging us to get a move on.

Bigmama brushed dirt from the front of her dress. "Grande Red planned this. She lured the dauphine to a shop with a tunnel that ends right here. She kidnapped him from the room under the stairs and dragged him down this tunnel to emerge the same way we have. She chose this spot. Why?"

Chapter 21

The answer to Bigmama's question seemed obvious. You couldn't emerge from the tunnel without staring straight at the pedestrian bridge. Its arch rose into the air taller than the massive concrete wharf beside the river, taller than anything around us. Other than the naval station, it was the tallest structure in the Bywater, which enforced height restrictions mostly through noisy peer pressure.

"Grande Red brought the dauphine here to show him the city." I walked toward the bridge, picking up my pace until I was loping like a wounded wolf. "She can't threaten him. He was ready to chunk himself off the rampart for his ideals. She has to threaten something he loves. That's the city. You heard him say that thing when we first arrived on the rampart."

"What thing?" Bigmama asked.

At the railroad tracks, I flung out my arm to halt the group. The train clacked up and down the tracks unpredictably. One time an impatient biker slid his bicycle between the coupled cars, unaware a stopped train doesn't whistle when it revs back up. The bike—plus the boy—got squashed. He lived, but you do not mess with the train. Coast clear, I let my group pass.

"He said something like Jesus wanting to tuck Jerusalem under his wing like a chicken, except the dauphine was talking about his cape or something. I can't remember exactly, but it was pro-New Orleans, same as Jesus loved Jerusalem."

The three of them stared at me as if they'd never heard of this man named Jesus.

None of my grannies had taught me religion. Tippy taught me how to gut a bream of its glistening roe, roll the fish in cornmeal, then bob it in a lake of Crisco in an iron skillet. Elfy taught me to lift the rubber stopper from the garbage disposal and stick my hand, sight unseen, into the black hole and retrieve lemon rinds, never flinching against my fear the disposal blades would spontaneously whir. Bigmama taught me to hate a semicolon.

With that background, I groped for something in community college that could hold my attention, and found religion. Well, religion and math. But the shock that sparked through me when I walked into the calculus room and intuited the answer to a lengthy equation scrawled on the chalkboard—that was religious too. I found more meat in World Religions than you would've thought possible in a Mississippi community college. In fact, now that I considered it, my religion fascination could be giving me this fever dream of St. Claude and his dauphine. Be careful, kids. Declare your major wisely.

We climbed to the top of the arch where we spread out, searching the Bywater for a sign of the dauphine or Grande Red or her minions. Below and off to the side was the trap door where we exited the tunnel. From this vantage point, you could see a sign poked in the ground. Warning! Tunnel Closed To The Public!

Following my gaze, Tip-Top said, "She emerged from the castle and, spying this high spot, walked straight down the street. She saw the sign. She didn't scout out the shop. She back-followed the tunnel. Never assume the order in which you discover information is the same as your enemy's."

"Tricky." I rested my elbows on the guardrail. A young mother talking on the phone pushed a jogging stroller down the park path. The bronze bell in the church tower rang eight times in the dusky air. I pivoted, scanning. Streetlights popped on up and down St. Claude Avenue. End-of-the-day traffic stacked up on the Claiborne Avenue bridge that crossed the Industrial Canal to the Lower Ninth Ward. All normal. No sign of the dauphine. I wasn't sure exactly what I was looking for. The dauphine strapped to a rooftop? The minions hunched over a prostrate body? A curling column of smoke?

Wait. Where was the castle?

Elfy tapped my arm. The baby's head lolled in the backpack, asleep, drool seeping down his chin.

"If you live nearby, we need to go," she said. "We can start again tomorrow."

"Go? We can't quit now. We haven't accomplished a damn thing."

"We know who our enemy is. We understand her reasoning." Elfy stroked the baby's smooth cheek. "That is the important thing in a hunt: know our prey. Now, come. We are exhausted."

I let her lead me by the hand toward the stairs. How we would, "start again tomorrow," I had no idea. But I silently followed my bedraggled krewe back to solid ground.

—

Midnight, I woke up on the sofa, disoriented and needing to pee. Finished in the bathroom, I peeked in the bedroom to check on Elfy and the baby. Not there. Tip-Top was still on her side of the bed, her unsheathed bowie knife on the bedside table. I returned to the sitting room where I'd slept (bathroom, bedroom, sitting room—that was my exorbitantly-priced loft). Just Bigmama, honking like a goose in the overstuffed chair.

With no sign of Elfy or the baby, I quietly slipped through the front door, careful not to jingle the bell I had hung on the knob to worn of intruders, and entered the dark hall.

Chapter 22

I was about to take the elevator to the lobby when I glanced down the wide hallway. At the end where the enormous picture window looked out on the river, Elfy lifted the baby over her head. The boy was silhouetted against the night, reflected in the opaque glass. A ghost child, thrilled with the ride and laughing in a deep chortle that echoed off the cement floor and brick walls. Timeless.

As I eased down beside Elfy on the bench, she resettled the baby in her lap. He grasped her thumb, curling it in his fingers. The tip turned red in his grip. Elfy wiggled her thumb, but the baby dauphine giggled and gripped tighter. Elfy slumped against the bench back, pretending to faint. Her swan neck curved against the blue velvet. She wore a pair of man-pajamas I had bought one night drunk-surfing the internet: maroon and white striped under a loosely belted maroon robe. With her black curls piled on her shoulders and her dark lashes brushing her cheeks, she could have been a plucky heroine of the 1940s as easily as her own 1840s, even the soon-to-be 2040s. Had we women really changed so little in two hundred years?

Without an opponent in his game, the dauphine released her thumb.

Elfy's lips curled in success. She knew how to control men, no matter the age.

"The baby was fussy and unable to sleep," Elfy said, reviving herself. "I didn't want to wake the others. Mrs. Daniels, in particular, was exhausted. She can't get much rest snoring like that. And Lord knows Mrs. Smith sleeps too lightly, knife at the ready." She smiled briefly. "Maybe it's me who wasn't able to sleep. Hard to relax after an argument. I replay the whole thing in my head over and over. Points I should have made. I'm much cleverer in hindsight."

Unaware, I had happily drifted off to sleep cocooned among my faux grannies. Such was life, lulling you into a sense of peace then—pow!—sucker punch. "You and Bigmama were fighting?"

Elfy set the baby on the carpet where he batted at the swirling pattern. "No, Mrs. Smith. I suggested a knife around a baby might not be a good idea. She said the knife had been at her side since she was fifteen years old, and three times it had saved her life. I don't know about the other two, but she described in unnecessary detail the one in her kitchen." She shuddered. "The very idea of a man's glistening intestines spilling out like the egg sac of a gutted fish."

Tip-Top wasn't my Tippy, but fish-gutting must have passed down same as killing.

"Anyway, she had good cause. No one wants to be attacked in their home. God knows during the war we had men crawling all over us. They'd shimmy up the gutters to the attic and appear in the hallway. Swaying, leering. Searching for food but thinking they'd found so much more." She chuckled. "You can throw men off guard more quickly with unexpected happiness than with anger. They wind up tossing their own selves down the stairs."

She shifted to face me. "But that's the exception. Violence is a failure."

"You're good with manipulation," I said, remembering my own violent reaction when my boss brushed up against me. "Most aren't."

"Manipulating women is hard. Our motives are too . . . webbed. Men are easy. Their emotions fly in one direction, and they aren't nimble. When caught unawares, they tend to be flat-footed, predictable. Servants to their feelings. I watched my sons grow up healthy children and emerge from puberty . . . different. Have you ever seen an abandoned dirtdobbers' nest?" She curved her fingers into an open interlocking ball. "The dirt is riven with empty tunnels where the larvae once nested. The walls are paper thin, they crumble at the touch. That was my sons. They constructed chambers in their brains to wall off their emotions, but the slightest provocation . . ." She poofed her fingers.

Gently she pulled the baby's fine silky curls, watching them rebound. "It took them leaving for me to see they needed help learning to handle their emotions. I thought it came as naturally to them as it does to us. I vowed to do better when they returned. Then they died in a war because the entire South couldn't control its emotions. Violence should always be a last resort, not a first. Mrs. Smith disagreed. The knife stayed on the table."

I wondered if Elfy had left the apartment due to her frustration with the argument or if she was furious she couldn't make Tip-Top do what she wanted. If she was anything like my Elfy, her softness was a weapon. Be disarming, let your opponent underestimate you. Then go for the jugular. "Tip-Top is very straightforward," I said.

Gazing out the picture window where the moon cast a glimmer across the river, she said, "I remember her from the blast."

Chapter 23

"Mrs. Smith's face was the last thing I saw in life." Elfy touched her cheek, remembering. "She wasn't happy to be on the podium—antsy and embarrassed. Mrs. Daniels was comfortable in the spotlight reading her poem, very dignified. She'd just gotten to an interesting part comparing mothers to reluctant warriors when Mrs. Smith turned her head to the side. Surprise blanked her face. Then it switched to recognition followed by horror. As if she'd suspected something all along and now understood it in a literal flash. We'd been set up to be immolated."

"Oh—no," I said and told Elfy the full story about the racist Red Shirts, their man Monger, and the startled horse. "It was an accident. Terrible, but an accident. Y'all were unintended casualties."

Elfy was quiet, considering this new interpretation. Her own life had been full of "accidental" death. She seduced her brother-in-law right up to the point of screwing him—grateful palm to her cheek, breathy murmurings of devotion—so he would argue her case for free, taking it all the way to the Mississippi Supreme Court and, against all odds, winning.

Unfortunately, he also fell hopelessly, helplessly in love. He wouldn't back off. Furious at his mooning, Elfy told her sister he was acting inappropriately and refused to allow him to cross the threshold of the house he had saved. He committed suicide. Though my Elfy wouldn't say how, I gathered it involved a pistol. Her sister lost her mind blaming Elfy for the death of her husband. Why had she maligned a good man who only wished to help? And what about Elfy's own husband. What had Elfy done to chase Gerald all the way back home? But none of that showed in Elfy's clear face.

"My son the politician thought he had landed on a can't lose idea: honor our beloved mothers," she finally said. "But as usual, we women just got in the way. Oopsie."

The baby dauphine grabbed Elfy's pajama trousers and pulled himself upright. Surprise and delight suffused his face.

"You'll be walking soon. Your greatest accomplishment, and you won't even remember it." She smiled at the baby with such tenderness it broke my heart.

"You laid eyes on this baby less than twelve hours ago, and you love him."

"My Delores was my missing coin." She ran her finger along his jaw line but swiftly retreated when he grabbed for it. He rubbed his forefinger and thumb together, greedy for more Elfy. "I had four children I dearly loved, only one of whom survived the war to adulthood, but the baby I lost . . . My whole body rebelled, refusing to believe that what we had spent nine months creating was dead, and I was the one who killed it."

"Oh, no," I said.

"Oh, yes. My despair killed it. The news of my husband's death sliced into me like a sword, rupturing the baby's placenta. Useless despair. We grieve lost things more than we rejoice at what we have."

The worn out baby had collapsed against her knee. He

smelled sweet as cotton candy. Elfy lifted him, limp in his sleep. She had dressed him for bed in one of my shirts. Ironic, but pretty accurate, to see him in a T-shirt for Jump, Little Children, a band my mom followed like a groupie. Outside the picture window, past the flood wall, the railroad tracks were filled with cars gray as clouds. Beyond that, the park's serpentining path, the batture of land exposed when the river retreated, and finally the river itself. Layered and complicated, like the city.

"Elfy, who brought Grande Red to life?" I asked. St. Claude had claimed he brought my grannies, but I think he was exaggerating. He didn't know them to bring them back. I expect he saw them in my brain where they appeared as soon as the looming castle signaled I was on an adventure. He then jumped on them as potential familiars. But I didn't know Grande Red. I couldn't have brought her to the city. "I really don't want to think random folks can enter this vision outside my control. I can't stand that."

She shook her head. "No, I doubt that's the case. The saint told us the vision was birthed by a poem you made up. What was it again?"

After I recited the ditty, she said, "Proceeding in order, you've got the royal dauphine, the burgundy, the rampart, and St. Claude. What you don't have is the beginning. Grande Red has something to do with what the ancient charters decree."

I slumped. It made sense, but where did it get me? "I don't know how I'm supposed to find the dauphine tomorrow. It's not like we have clues to follow or breadcrumbs or anything. He just vanished."

"Don't you worry." She patted my hand. "You'll wake up, and it will all be clear."

It peeved me, her tone, even the gentle hand pat. Just like my Elfy when she was trying to convince me an impossible situation would work itself out. No, not trying to convince me. Smugly assuring me, as if she knew the secret workings of the universe. Worse, I couldn't remember a time when she had been wrong. Whatever had sent me to my room weeping—whether it was a cold certainty that I was the only girl in the class who wouldn't be invited to Maureen Stouffer's party or the hot shame of being cut in the first round of tryouts for the varsity basketball team—it always worked out. Often because Elfy secretly intervened to make sure that an invitation came in the mail. Other times, through the cruel intervention of fate. I was "called up" to the basketball squad after half the girls died when a drunk driver hit the team bus.

"Maybe if I knew more about him," I protested. The dauphine obviously had a complicated relationship with the lanky red-headed assassin. Which meant whatever happened next probably had to do with their personal history, of which I was ignorant. "But I don't. Which means he could be anywhere."

"No, he can only be where he is." Elfy stood, grunting from the dead weight of the sleeping child. "And you will know where that is tomorrow."

The baby's eyes opened as Elfy settled him on her shoulder. He watched me trail them back to the apartment. He could walk. I'd seen him. He just preferred to have Elfy carry him. His gaze tracked my movement. Making sure I followed.

Part IV

Going About it A Different Way

Chapter 24

Bacon popped and sizzled as Bigmama ran a fork around the iron skillet. She had taken over making breakfast while Elfy sat on the futon entertaining the baby. Beside them, Tip-Top cleaned her suede boots with a dishrag, knife by her side. Earlier, she had brandished the knife when opening the door to a knock. It was the apartment manager wanting to change the AC filter. Tip-top suggested she come back later. Served her right. My apartment's motto (yes, it had a motto: Be Cool!) had always struck me as a threat. Sooner or later, I would do something to make the manager declare I wasn't being cool, and tear up my lease. Maybe she'd think twice now.

Tip-Top had removed her leather belt, but otherwise she'd slept in her clothes. Bigmama wore my fluffy white robe. Grease from the bacon spotted the robe's sleeve. In my world, Tippy was the cook. And when I was in Jackson it was Elfy, never Bigmama. I reminded myself these women were not the grandmothers who raised me. They moved comfortably around each other as if their mutual death made them intimates. After all, what could they do to misstep, offend, or negligently disrespect each other? They'd blown up together. Truth tell, even though I had thoroughly screwed up my quest, losing one dauphine and gaining another, I couldn't describe how thankful I was to have my murderous grannies returned to me, pre-incarnated.

Back when I was in the ninth grade and Elfy and Bigmama died so close together—pow, pow!—I spent hours on the porch glider staring into space, searching the air for the slot they'd disappeared through. I stared so hard it felt as if I were swirling down the bathtub drain—weak, thin, unable to fight back. I was on the glider because I was afraid of the house. At dusk I had opened the screen door and stood between it and the kitchen door, listening for Elfy to wave me in or Bigmama to shoo me on out. When neither appeared, I slept on cushions sour with mildew and watched stars spin across the sky while I pretended their light wove a net that rocked Elfy and Bigmama the same way the glider rocked me.

When I finally slept, I dreamed the kitchen pipes burst and water gushed down the hallway flooding the house, rising higher and higher. I tried to lap it up, but it was foamy with dust and splinters, and I cut my tongue. I woke hot and itchy under the blanket, dry mouthed.

Twenty-four hours in, when my empty stomach made me brave the kitchen, my footsteps startled a big gray rat waddling across the linoleum. It reared onto its hind legs, showing its jiggly testicles, then shot forward, chasing me out the door. The next morning when I came in from the porch, I was armed. I swung the shovel and batted the rude rat against the wall, scooped it up, and flung it into the street where it was immediately squished under the wheels of a pickup. I shoveled it into a hole in the garden, wondering if the carcass would sprout into a rhino or hippo or another large gray creature that would take its revenge on me.

Only time would tell.

I cried myself to sleep in that empty house, wishing my careless parents had died instead of my grannies. Of course, when they did die two years later—pow, pow!—things got even worse.

My parents were the drunk drivers who took out the girls' basketball team.

No, they didn't do it on purpose, committing double suicide to catapult me onto the team. They didn't even know I played basketball. They had six DUIs between them and had lost their driver's licenses years earlier. Though the scope of the accident was horrifying, the fact of it was just a matter of time.

I became notorious. Kids spit on me in the hall. They threaded notes through the slats in my locker urging me to join my parents and off myself, their hateful words smeared with boogers. It was too much. I took to screaming at night. I woke up to find Tippy standing beside the bed. She was draped in her old popcorn spread, her eyes bugged at my distress. "Demons," she whispered, but the library books said it was night terrors brought on by stress. Well, yeah.

Now the ghost ancestors of the women whose deaths had shredded my life were serving me eggs and sliding up to my table for breakfast. The constant whine of a TV seeped from the apartment next door. Through the opposite wall came the clunk, clunk, clunk of heavy weights dropped between reps. I'd seen the dude in that apartment. Far be it from me to body shame, but let's just say he could use a new routine.

Turned out, the baby dauphine could say a few words—"up," "down," "mine." Earlier, we'd played "gimme" with my sword. Now he scooted his booty across the concrete floor, circling Elfy, who smiled at him indulgently. The others watched me gobble my bacon and drain my orange juice—when was the last time I'd eaten a traditional breakfast? The women didn't partake. Apparently, when you're called back from the dead, food doesn't work for you.

Focused as always, Tip-Top wanted to know our plans for

the day. As I scraped and washed my plate, she paced the tiny living area. My sword clanged against the sink. Whatever spell was controlling us had allowed me to change into my pajamas for the night, but when I'd woken, I was re-garbed in my red jumpsuit. It was disconcerting. The jumpsuit was awesome, but a woman liked to be in charge of her own clothes. To prove I could, I re-tied the dauphine's cape around my neck.

Leaning against the counter, I wiped my hands on a dish towel. "I was thinking, what if we've been looking at this all wrong? I've been treating the dauphine as a victim. Drunk on the rampart. Kidnapped by Grande Red. Forced down the tunnel and threatened with his life. But we all want to control our own lives, right?" I fanned my cape to the side, Batman-style. "What if the dauphine is more of an actor than I've given him credit for?"

"You think he's role-playing? Pretending to be someone he's not?" Elfy frowned, obviously unhappy with this interpretation.

"Not an actor as in Shakespeare." I dropped my cape. "An actor as in having a say-so. Agency, we call it now. What if he's working his kidnapper, trying to persuade Grande Red to his side?"

Chapter 25

Tip-Top wanted to know how that insight helped us. If I had inherited the woman's focus, I would be queen of the world. A flicker ignited in my brain. Could this entire experience be designed to show me the positive aspects of my ancestors? Not only to identify with their killer instincts, but to value their other contributions to our family line?

This startling idea threw me off, blanking my brain. "What was I saying?" I asked.

"Explaining your theory on the dauphine and Grande Red," Tip-Top said, retaking a seat at the kitchen table. She rested her balled fists on the tabletop, which made it wobble because it was held up by wooden piers scavenged after Katrina washed away the houses they once supported. If Tip-Top had worn a watch, she'd have been checking the time, wanting me to get on with it.

"Right. The first thing the dauphine said up on the rampart was how much he loved New Orleans. So Grande Red takes him to the arch where she can threaten him with harm to the city. How does he respond? By convincing her to love the city as much as he does."

A thought struck me. When I first came to New Orleans, I had been on a tear to learn everything I could about my new home. I started in Jackson Square, seated on a pew at St. Louis Cathedral as Mass unfolded. Then I migrated next door to the Cabildo where I snoozed through its portraits of dead White men in gold braid until I stumbled across Napoleon's death mask. I mean, a mask made of the man's face while his body was still warm. Molded by the doc who split him open for autopsy. That made me flee to the Voodoo Museum on Dumaine where I stood in line with the true believers to light a candle for my dead grannies and, reluctantly, a skinny candle for my parents. I quit my touring after the Historic New Orleans Collection informed me the entire New World was colonized based on weird obsessions—in the case of New Orleans, tobacco.

But the most important thing I learned was that just because Thomas Jefferson bought New Orleans as part of the Louisiana Purchase, don't think the city considered itself American. The majority of New Orleanians kept speaking French. They fought in the streets with their American neighbors. They elected Frenchman after Frenchman as mayor. The last French mayor, Louis Philippe de Roffignac, was a real party animal who went out with a bang.

"He knew all the French royalty," I explained to my grannies. "He kept up a steady stream of dukes and duchesses traipsing to New Orleans for balls. It almost bankrupted the city, but Roffie didn't care. Guess who was his favorite French visitor? The one who came to town more than any other?"

"The king?" Bigmama guessed.

"No, the king was probably home working. But his son . . ."

"The dauphin?" Elfy stared down at the baby in her arms who blew spit bubbles at her.

"Not just any dauphin. The last dauphin of France."

I could see the wheels turning as my Mississippi grannies tried to get onboard with this French thing. Never mind that the

French dauphine had been with us since the moment they appeared in the castle. And the French St. Claude called them back. Into a city named New Orleans.

"And you believe this last dauphin is the one we should have protected?" Tip-Top asked.

Her throwing my failure in my face irked me, but all I said was, "Yes, I do."

"So our dauphine visited New Orleans and fell in love, same as my Jewel." Bigmama rubbed her chin like my high school geometry teacher pondering a complicated formula. "When she was fourteen, Jewel and another little girl rode a steamer to New Orleans. They were meant to be attending a tent revival. The child was a foot-washing Baptist and, predictably, a horrible influence on Jewel. They absconded to sin city, and when they returned, my daughter declared she intended to move there. She stuck to it, too, until she got into a fight with the foot-washer and decided she detested everything they had in common. If the dauphine kept running away to New Orleans, maybe he, too, wants to stay. Avoid assuming the throne, never become king of France at all."

"Or maybe, as king, he would direct France's riches toward his beloved New Orleans, and the greedy ones who covet the money for themselves, such as Grande Red, wish him dead." Elfy spoke as she swung the dauphine's arms back and forth, which made him lean back, face to the ceiling, and giggle.

"Or maybe Grande Red is the kin of a man the dauphine has insulted, and she pursues the dauphine to take her revenge," Tip-Top offered.

"Wait, wait, wait, wait, wait." I batted aside their theories—each of which mirrored their own lives—and opened my laptop. Hurriedly, I typed in, "last dauphine of France." A list of women popped up. So I backspaced the e. The men showed. I scrolled to the end while Tip-Top peered over my shoulder. I hated people peering over my shoulder. Just ask my dead boss. I glanced back at her to signal this was rude behavior. Her gaze was fixed on the scrolling page, a mix of fear and fascination.

"The internet. Just like an encyclopedia but bigger." I pointed to the last entry: Louis Antoine, Duke of Angouleme, the last Dauphin of France.

We read the meager sentences. He abdicated the throne and died of old age in exile. He was known as "the twenty-minute king."

"Bet the women teased him about that," I mumbled, wondering if the information in Wikipedia would change depending on what happened today, tomorrow, the next day.

"I agree with Etoile. I believe the dauphine is trying to persuade Grande Red to share his love of the city." Bigmama removed her journal and made notes as she spoke. "For reasons we can only guess at, Grande Red sees the dauphine as a threat to the throne. Her fanatical devotion to the monarchy has pushed her beyond the bounds of reason. A latter-day Joan of Arc who takes the fate of the nation into her own hands, but without St. Joan's religious guidance. And more underhanded. A back-alley Joan of Arc."

Her obsession with Joan of Arc made me wonder if Bigmama was the ancestor who had traveled abroad and returned with the marble bust of St. Joan that my Elfy lovingly wiped with her chambray cloth. I could absolutely see Bigmama threatening her progeny to keep the bust with them always.

"She plotted against the dauphine and was lurking in the shadows when you called him to New Orleans," Bigmama continued. "Swept up as if in a tornado, she pursues him still. The dauphine hopes that showing her his love of the city will break through her obsession and melt her cruel heart."

She halted to jot a note, and I envisioned her writing "cruel heart melts."

It was unnerving to have Bigmama agree with me. She had been wrong about Grande Red creating the tunnel. Her current narrative of the dauphine/Grande Red story was pure romanticism, same as the frothy, lying novels she wrote. But my

Tippy had a saying about blind squirrels and acorns.

The best way to lure someone over to your side was to show them your love of something—your dog, your roses, deep dish pizza. It was why married men intent on seduction instinctively showed off photos of their wives and children, which seemed counterintuitive. But they knew that appearing to be loving made them more lovable. Plus, the dauphine absolutely would believe he could talk poor benighted Grande Red out of her obsession, easy peasy. After all, he was a man.

"So where in New Orleans is guaranteed to kindle love for the city?" I mused. "Where has the dauphine taken Grande Red?"

Chapter 26

"It will be a place he's familiar with, correct?" Bigmama said, as the screeching of the Bywater train pierced the apartment's hurricane-proof windows. Elfy covered her ears while Tip-Top studied the ceiling. Outside, the wind had picked up, and clouds swept inland as if we were on a ship sailing the seas. My logical, plot-writing grandmother continued, unperturbed. "An older part of the city still extant from the days when the dauphine visited."

"Not sure when that was," I said, trying to remember the dates on the Wiki page. "Mid-1820s, I think? The safest bet would be the French Quarter."

Elfy bounced the baby on her knees. "Let me tell you about my oldest child, Joe. When he was eight years old, Joe would sit on the rug in the greeting hall and play for hours. Blocks and toy soldiers. But his favorite thing was building card houses. He would add one more story on top of another. They fell. Always, they fell because they were flimsy creations, constructed purely from his imagination."

Bigmama glared at her. "You don't agree with my theory?"

Elfy wrapped her arms around the baby and squeezed him to her breast. "I think the most dangerous thing a person can do is convince themselves they understand another's relationship."

"And how is that relevant to this discussion?"

"I am not going to waste time explaining something I sense is outside your understanding."

These two were being exactly like my own Bigmama and Elfy, trading barbs over long-ago hurts, attacking each other's deficiencies to do their damage. What we needed now was action.

"Do we have to do this, guys? Whatever's going on, Grande Red intends—intended . . ." I wasn't sure how the timeline worked. Were Grande Red and the dauphine mere spirits? Or were they visitors from the past who could return to their time and alter the future?

I shook my head to clear it. It didn't matter, the point remained the same.

"Grande Red intends to harm the dauphine. Elfy, do you have a better plan?"

"I am perfectly happy to follow you, Etoile, wherever you believe the dauphine might be." She pressed the baby's cheek to hers and avoided Bigmama's gaze shooting darts.

"I want to go to Jackson Square," I answered.

The first time I laid eyes on Jackson Square, I thought I'd somehow crossed the Atlantic into a European city. Its broad plaza and cathedral spire were postcard perfect Frenchiness. "If he's not there, we'll broaden our search. But right now, we need to act quick. Grande Red has probably plotted this whole thing out. She literally tricked us with smoke and mirrors," I said, remembering the fog machine she'd set to running in the storage room. She delayed us then positioned herself below to capture the dauphine. "She's the type of sneak who might crawl into a public ceremony and plant an explosive charge beneath a podium. And blow up the speaker. And various dignitaries," I added in case they hadn't gotten it.

Ignoring me, Tip-Top glanced at her pajamaed companions. "Five minutes, we move out."

Later, as I was locking the apartment behind us, Elfy held me back, her face stern.

"Etoile, you had good cause. You wanted to prod us into action, and I understand that. God knows I've employed certain tactics beyond the point of decency." Her gaze flickered, but she kept going. "However, in the future, please don't use the sensitive subject of our deaths to win a point. It's disrespectful."

Relief rushed through me—that was all?—and I quickly apologized. "I'm so sorry. I won't do it again."

Elfy raised on tiptoe and kissed me on my cheek. "I am on your side, child. Whether you want me or not."

Chapter 27

New Orleans might be famous for its nightlife, but native New Orleanians live for the day. They rise with the sun and stay outside as long as humanly possible. I swear they act like this whole diurnal thing is a joke—ha, ha. If they just keep jogging the levee or kayaking Bayou St. John or make one last ascent up City Park's Laborde Mountain (elevation forty-three feet), they can lock the sun in the sky. Finally, they have to admit the time has come to retire, at least until the next morning when day breaks like a dropped china plate: sharp, deadly, but everyday common.

The rooster crowed on Montegut Street.

The sun blasted across the Bywater rooftops.

Before we got out of the parking lot, the drift of coffee from the roasting warehouse on N. Peters brought my ragtag group to a full, caffeinated stop. After pausing to enjoy the scent, we turned upriver toward the Quarter, joining the flow of folks heading to jobs and school or to save their cross-gendered doppelgänger from his nemesis.

"How far are we from the Quarter?" Tip-Top asked.

Tip-Top had to know the city. She had lived in an area of the state that sucked up to Louisiana like a piglet clamping onto its mama's teat. Surely she would've considered New Orleans part of her world, just across the river. Same went for Bigmama in Vicksburg and even Elfy in Jackson. That entire corner of the South collapsed into New Orleans. But maybe weird transportation made casual visiting totally whacked back then.

"Raise your hand if you've ever been to New Orleans before," I said to the group, walking backward to see the results.

Only the baby raised his arm.

So maybe I was back-reading my current world into theirs, which jiggled my confidence. But what could you do? I hadn't time to figure it out. Just relax and enjoy being with my grannies on their first trip to New Orleans.

"We're about half a mile from the Quarter," I told Tip-Top, directing them across Homer Plessy Street, where a long-necked crane stood by the railroad tracks like an old-fashioned traveling salesman assessing his mark. We would follow Chartres Street through the Faubourg Marigny to Esplanade Avenue, then jog over to Royal Street. (I wanted to avoid the eighteenth century Old Ursuline Convent on Chartres. My group might not react well to a place where the rooms for the women were called cells.) From Royal, we would hit Dauphine Street to come around to Jackson Square.

The wind blew, and a palm tree curved like a woman bending her neck to rinse suds from her hair. One by one, we swerved to avoid where tree roots buckled the sidewalk. I glanced over my shoulder then shook off the paranoid feeling that someone was following us. I swear the baby rolled his eyes at me.

We walked into shadows thrown by overhanging oaks and back into sunlight. I wondered how my grannies were seeing my city. Was the graffiti public art or vandalism? I had part of my answer when Tip-Top shied away from a fantastic mural of a girl growing into a tree. She grimaced as if the painting were the underworld breaking through. The Tip-Top line had always been more inclined to functional mechanics than foolishness, but her reaction to the mural still disappointed.

Bigmama seemed interested in the writers scribbling beneath a coffee shop's red umbrellas. But did she see them fermenting creativity or being lazy? When she turned her attention to the buttermilk clouds scuttling across the sky, I wondered if she was like me, believing the wind held answers, the clouds its alphabet? When she caught me looking, she said, "Something smells funny."

Elfy was my last chance. Of all my own grannies, she was the only one who had what you'd call whimsy. Was she focused on the unsightly potholes filled with milk crates? Or was she enthralled by the magenta blossoms prancing down the iron fence like samba dancers? A gust blew, and leftover Mardi Gras beads tinkled from the branches of an orange tree to land at her feet. She ignored the offering, and my heart sank.

Yet, something told me if the grannies knew I wanted them to love my city as much as I did, they'd be tripping all over themselves to make it happen. Bigmama would be admiring the bright yellows in the mural. Tip-Top would be praising the ingenuity of the milk-crated potholes, and Elfy would be scooping up filthy beads left and right. Not just to show they cared for me. Working to outdo each other. Part of it was natural competitiveness, like my own grannies. But something else lurked between them. A lingering suspicion, as if the others were complicit in the explosion that wiped them from the face of the earth. Whatever, they seemed to rise to the bait of each other.

My pace had slowed, and I realized I was dragging my feet, disappointed at the group for not feeling my city. Me and my pitiful self, glomming onto my new family. I was the only child of two only children. I had no cousins, no aunts, no uncles. My place in the world had always been as tenuous as the small saffron-colored teeth I found in Mother's costume jewelry box. My baby teeth. I had held one up to the light. The top was tinged brown, the tip translucent. Tooth Fairy horde. I sifted the buttons and jewelry. Three teeth. That sounded about right. The Tooth Fairy had been hit or miss in my house. But why even keep the teeth? Sentiment? Or had she felt disloyal tossing them into the metal garbage can along with the clouds of hair from her hairbrush and used tampons rolled in tissue paper? Or maybe it was just proof I had been her child, she my mother. The blip before the end. I was the last of the descendants of my faux grannies. After me, the lines would disappear.

    I kicked the tip of my sword. What was it with this hallucination, anyway? Who cared if we rescued a privileged prince from a mean-ass woman and her galumphing tribe of bullies? If the adventure wasn't going to be fun, I didn't want any part of it. Things had better pick up soon, or I was outta here.

Chapter 28

Amazingly enough, we attracted little attention as we crossed Elysian Fields Avenue single file, our very own Abby Road, except three of the four of us were actually dead, plus baby. A guy riding a unicycle yelled at Elfy, "Hey, mama!" and she happily waved back. Bigmama snorted, and Elfy stuck out her tongue at her. Bigmama said, "Your child is what smells."

"He smells like a baby," Elfy hiked the child on her hip and scooted past the ghost bike memorial erected on the neutral ground. Bigmama retrieved her journal and scratched something as if plotting revenge against Elfy. Tip-Top shot daggers at them both. We were fraying at the edges. I could only thank God they hadn't coalesced into a united front against me . . . yet.

A second line was squirreling into Washington Square, which was probably why no one was paying attention to us. Like a lot of second lines, the narrow front had expanded as random who's-its joined in. The parade was now a funnel of writhing bodies, mostly White people. Which meant it wasn't actually a true second line, just someone's idea of a party. The front tip of the line, which might have told me what was being celebrated, was lost in the park's forest of live oaks.

A bicycle bell sounded in frustration at the lump of revelers. We, too, needed to get on the other side of the mob, but my energy flagged, worn out with how pissy my grannies were being. Rather than fight our way forward, I sat on the curb to wait it out, adjusting the sword so it wouldn't trip anyone. The grannies backed up to the park fence to watch the parade surge by

On Elysian Fields, angry drivers honked at the revelers, many of whom happily shot the bird in reply. A White chick rattled a tambourine and whooped, dancing across the street. Moisture from the river hung heavy in the air. That and the smell of salty popcorn. A red vendor's cart had appeared, magically drawn by the throng of people. As it squeaked by, I wondered if the concrete I sat on would pick the seat of my red jumper and leave fuzzy pills. Make my bum look ragged.

"Etoile?"

I glanced up.

St. Claude frowned down at me.

Chapter 29

"Hey, you!" I grinned like a fool, way too excited to see the besainted one. "How's it going? I didn't know you were coming back. Wanna go with us to Jackson Square? We can get a Lucky Dog, my treat."

"Why do you have an eighteen-month-old dauphine with you?" St. Claude asked, his gaze riveted on Elfy and the baby. In the distance, the thumping drums and blasting horns of a marching band rolled in our direction. When it arrived, we would be engulfed in a mad sea of noise.

"You recognize him, huh? And you know how old he is?" I squinted up at the saint, impressed. Babies were like blobs of playdough to me, squishy and fun but not beings with actual ages.

St. Claude sniffed dismissively. "I have known him since the day he was born. I can tell you how many teeth he has in his mouth right now."

The saint bared his teeth at the babe who reciprocated, transforming his cherubic countenance into that of a demon.

Not backing down, Claude expanded into a pufferfish of superiority which caused the baby to raise his arms like a tiny strongman. I would almost pay money to see them battle it out—my favorite saint and the only baby I'd ever connected with—but a question was tickling my brain. I admit things had been hectic recently, and I'd forgotten the saint was listening in on my life. But given that, shouldn't he know the whole story of the baby?

Claude shifted uncomfortably, clearly reading my thoughts.

I crossed my legs, settling in on the gritty streets of New Orleans. "So, spill it. If you've been spying on me, why don't you know how we got the little dauphine?"

Claude pretended to be engrossed with the antics of a woman dressed as a lion who was prowling the edges of the throng, clawing at everyone she passed.

As I responded to his question—"All right, all right, we found the baby under a staircase and Elfy wanted to keep him so I let her"—the lion woman slapped Claude on the shoulder, distracting him. He brushed off the woman's paw and returned his attention to me.

"Again, I ask, why are you carting around a young dauphine?"

"I just told you," I said, and watched his mouth purse like someone had tugged on a drawstring. "Wait. Did you not just hear what I said?"

"The crowd is loud."

"But you should have heard it." I gave him a significant look.

"You humiliate me over the limitations of this?" He motioned with his hand down the length of his body. "The protruding stomach that cannot take food? Ears that can't hear, a mind that runs on the same track day and night, chasing answers that scamper away like blind mice? My will is not my own, and what is there to life other than controlling one's will? I am not alive. I am merely embodied."

At my silence, he threw up his hands in frustration. "Oh,

Etoile. Do I have to explain everything to you? It's embarrassing."

'Twas true. His papery cheeks had flushed pink. But I waited him out, thrumming my fingers on my knee, my rhythm instinctively syncing with the thumping of the approaching band.

"I am in your head," Claude finally said, refusing to meet my eye. His linen robe fluttered in the wind, and the seed pearls sewn into the hem clattered like small chittering birds. The man was sophistication incarnate. "The ramifications of that are obvious."

"Soooooo." I considered. "You hear what's going on in my head because you're in my head, but not what I say because you're not in my mouth? Cool."

"When you speak, your words cease being thoughts and become real. But no, actually not cool. If you were alone, your thoughts would flow as easily as a navigable stream. But with all those women around you, you've been talking nonstop. The moment between your thoughts and your speaking is too short. Your thoughts arrive like . . . what do they call that new tap-tap-a-tap-tap?" He tapped his forefinger in the air.

"Morse code?" I guessed.

"It is unintelligible. I hear assassin then foul talk of vomit and profane musings on killing rodents and boogers on letters. You really need to clean up your thoughts, Etoile."

"The better to keep you out of my head, my dear." I grinned as the crowd surged into the park. Surely the end of the second line would arrive soon. A clown with a daisy face approached our group and offered the baby a blue sno-ball, though Hansen's had closed for the season so the sno-ball was an impostor. Elfy sized up the clown but let it continue. The child poked his finger in the shaved ice and slurped.

"He's a cute kid," I said to the saint. "You should cut him some slack."

"I am not opposed to the baby, Etoile. It's the principles of this universe I am trapped in that make me fear for his presence. They can't run into each other, you know, he and the adult dauphine. They can't occupy the same space."

"What do you mean, 'occupy the same space'?"

"They can't lay eyes on each other."

"Oh." I envisioned me trying to pry the baby from Elfy's motherly fingers. "What happens if they do?"

"You tell me."

The saint stepped aside as a group of naked bicyclists wove around us. The straggler at the end rode a bike with a green paper-mache head of Godzilla jutting over the front wheel. Gold tinsel fluttered from Godzilla's mouth. A scaly tail crooked from the bike's back fender. It was stunning. I saluted the biker, paying homage. Briefly, I wished my life could go back to being normal where I had nothing better to do than admire the creative chaos of the city

I stood and brushed off my britches, ready to get going again.

"Claude, please quit being coy. What's going on here? Why can't the two dauphines meet up?"

Chapter 30

"Consider your own behavior," St. Claude said. Behind him the parade gyrated, and brass notes clean as the stropped edge of a knife split the air. "Being around these women you consider your grannies, has it left you an adult? Or have you regressed to the sniveling, complaining child you were when they wiped your bottom to ensure it was clean of poop?"

I pictured myself whining to my grannies who weren't even my real grannies, the pull of my childhood persona almost too strong to fight. Down the street, a siren signaled for the crowd to part for the marching band. My three grannies started almost in unison . . . amateurs. Otherwise, no one moved, and the siren ripped again—the crowds never pay attention until at least three rips. Quick, before the siren sounded again, I answered, "When you're around family, you regress."

"So will the dauphine. If he and the baby are in the same space, the baby will win out. He will absorb the adult dauphine, and only the baby will remain in this time."

"Oh man, that sucks."

The saint grimaced. "It would be intolerable. You simply can't do that to the dauphine. Years would pass before he again achieved the age of reason, which might technically be seven years old, but everyone who believes that, stand on their head."

I was struck with Claude's loyalty to the dauphine, who was tipping his blue sno-ball toward the ground. Elfy held him loosely around the waist but made no move to interfere with his play. She was good with him, easy. Letting him make his own mistakes, but never removing her hand from him. Ready to step in if it went too far. Despite my deep love for the grannies who raised me to be tough and self-reliant, I wondered what it would have been like to experience that soft, protective love.

"You said you knew the dauphine from birth. How is that?" I asked Claude.

The drum major's whistle shrilled—tweet! tweet! tweet! The crowd, which might ignore the police, knew better than to defy the drum major and high-stepping majorettes. Shuffling, they began to make way.

As if sensing the time to move on was nearing, the baby dropped his sno-ball face down on the sidewalk. A line of ants immediately diverted to the sticky treat.

Claude's face softened as he watched the child. "He entered this world an angel. Pure as snow, no trace of the soot of his mother. If it were not an affront to the Almighty, I'd swear on the King James the child was created as Venus: birthed from the brain rather than the womb of the woman who claimed to be his mamma. To think she now chases him through the public streets!"

"Chases him through the streets?" I leaped up and yelled to be heard over the band, which was almost upon us. "Are you saying Grande Red is the dauphine's mother?"

Chapter 31

After Claude and I sorted out that "Grande Red" was the nickname the store clerk had given the woman threatening to kill the dauphine, Claude confirmed that, yes indeed, Grande Red was the dauphine's mom. Not an obsessed Joan of Arc-ish anti-monarch, which meant Bigmama was batting zero.

"Holy crap," I said.

"Tell me about it." Claude checked the area around him as if he were taking his leave. "Imagine my surprise when I hear from you that the dauphine's assassin is a lanky redhead in black lace with whom he shared history. Of course, it does help explain why the Bywater chose you for this mission."

"It does?"

The saint, who had gathered the hem of his robe, halted his preparations.

"Etoile, you have as much experience with . . . odd mothering as anyone I know. Can you think of a better person to help the dauphine navigate a mother who consistently goes too far in pursuit of her goals?"

"But how did she arrive, Claude?" I remembered what Elfy had suggested. "Did the decree of the ancient Chartres bring the dauphine's mother to us?"

His eyes sparkled. "You are a constant surprise, my dear. Yes, the Duke of Chartres, Louis Philippe I, was hell-bent on restoring his monarchy following the Revolution. He succeeded when his cousin King Charles X abdicated during our recent July Revolution. Not satisfied, the Duke of Chartres decreed that Charles's son must also abdicate. Charles's son is our dauphine."

"Okaaaay."

"The Duke of Chartres is why the dauphine faces the dilemma he does: Shall he defy the Duke of Chartres and assume the throne? Or shall he acquiesce in the decree deposing him? His father insists he comply, his mother pleads with him to resist. Unseemly shouting ensues." The saint wagged his head in disapproval. "You can see why the queen considers the Duke of Chartres her sworn enemy."

I really had no idea what he was talking about.

"Personally, I think, given time, the queen could have forgiven the duke for dethroning her husband, but his insistence on dispossessing her son was too much. The queen does not suffer rebuke well. To answer your question, she is an integral part of this moment, and yes, I expect your rhyme referring to the decree brought her to New Orleans with us."

"And the baby?" I explained how Grande Red, like a demented stork, had deposited the baby dauphine under the stairs. "Did the rhyme call him back, too?"

"You interrupted us at a tense time, Etoile," the saint said as the band halted and marched in place, drums setting the tempo. "We were crowded into the smelly Tuileries Palace tower with its open latrine buckets. The king had signed the abdication only to have the duke send word he considered Charles yet a traitor if his son did not join the abdication. Outside the high window, the carpenters hammered up the guillotines. Not a threat, a promise. The Queen Mother was growing hysterical, clinging to the dauphine's arm, pleading with him to be the sweet child she had brought up, so handsome in his brocade jacket as he toddled proudly by her side. At that moment your ditty coiled its fist around us. I can only assume it swept her up with the remembered child clinging to her skirts, along with his nursemaids. But you have allowed yourself to be sidetracked by her. Do your job, and do it quickly. Get the dauphine to assume the throne."

"But the dauphine says if he rules, he dies. Now I see why. Defying the king—guillotines. Hey!" I shouted as the saint faded like Glinda the Good Witch of the North. "I don't agree on the whole assuming the crown thing. Did you get that? I'm not making choices for him, you hear?"

I wanted to jump up and down and shout at him to come back. But I needed to gather my grannies and the baby and get the hell out of the way. The parade had restarted with a lurch, and the drums were pounding, and the horns were quick whipping from side to side, and the girls carrying the banner wouldn't give way for nobody. I grabbed Elfy's hand and shouted for her to grab the others and stick together. The crush of people would whoosh us forward like a raging river. I was successfully leading us through the teeming masses when my brace caught on the iron fence.

I'd long ago traded my clunky brace for a molded blue one with a band that squirmed across the top of my shoe, sleek and modern. Too sleek. A fence stake was lodged between the strap and my shoe. I jerked at it, but that threatened to break the strap. If I didn't free it, the momentum of the crowd would break my skinny leg like a chicken bone.

I was opening my mouth to call for help when a man big as Sasquatch lunged from the gyrating crowd and slammed into me. I shoved him off. He staggered but couldn't go far because the crowd was holding him upright. His fatty eyelids drooped from drink.

"What's sa matter?" he asked. He wore a dark green fringed jacket and matching britches, which might have led to my Sasquatch impression . . . a Black Sasquatch in a top hat. A gator's claw dangled from the hat's brim.

"My foot!" I yelled in his ear.

He glared at Elfy who held onto me with one hand and pressed the baby to her breast with her other. "The baby yours?" he asked, as if he suspected her of having absconded with the child, which she kind of had.

Elfy blushed and ducked her head. Not embarrassed. Proud.

"My foot's stuck in the fence," I shouted at Sasquatch. "I can't bend down to get it out 'cause I can't let go of my friends. That foot." I jerked my head at the leg which thankfully wasn't the one where the sword lay. "Help me." I got it all out as quickly as I could to keep him from swishing back through the crowd.

Bending, he grabbed my ankle. "You got a metal foot," he said, twisting the calf and yanking my knee in an awkward angle.

"Be careful!" I hollered as he roughly pushed the foot down then up, ramming my knee into the fence and zinging pain. But the foot was freed.

"Got it!" he yelled into my ear, nearly busting my eardrum for absolutely no reason. The band had passed, the crowd with it.

"Thank you," I said and turned to urge my grannies to get a move on. We needed to free the dauphine and somehow persuade Grande Red and her minions to let him make his own decisions about life.

But Sasquatch grabbed my arm and flipped up my palm, flattening it. His touch was leathery as a monkey's paw.

"Best palm reader on Bourbon," he said, sweat popping on his upper lip. "Good week, I gross a thou, minimum."

Gently, he studied my palm. Concern clouded his eyes.

"Your future doesn't look good, lady. You got a bad moon rising over Mars. The red planet. Violence, negative energy.

Weird tools. Come see me for a full reading. I'll give you a discount."

He hustled away, and I was writing him off as a typical busker peddling whatever he had to sell, when the crowd parted and three women with flaring scarlet capes hurtled toward me, knives raised.

The baby gurgled, "Down, down!"

"The minions!" I cried. "The minions! Grande Red's minions!"

Chapter 32

In one swift move, Elfy shoved the baby at me. She dipped her slim fingers into the hidden pocket of her skirt and withdrew her pearl-handled pistol. Bigmama popped the head of her leather cudgel from her sash. Tip-Top's bowie knife glinted.

The three red-caped women screeched to a halt, tumbling all over each other.

They pointed and hooted at my grannies' weapons, believing them as fake as their own rubber knives. Their scarlet lips laughed open-mouthed as they flowed past us into the park.

My grannies and I pivoted and watched them disappear, harmless paraders. Women dressed for fun, not malice. In my arms, the baby waved. "Bye, bye. Bye, bye."

I shook my head, trying to clear the image I'd had of evil-eyed minions intent on killing.

As the rest of us stood stupidly, Tip-Top took charge. She led us through the parade stragglers and down Royal into the hive of the Quarter. At the intersection of Royal and Governor Nicholls, rain began to fall from the almost-clear sky as if dripping through a leaky colander. My entourage glanced upward, puzzled. But wait—in a minute, the rain would stop. Not like the days when the rain fell in PTSD-inducing sheets that backed up sewers, ate the streets, turned passing cars into weapons of wave destruction that kicked ripples through front doors. Sky, rain, the Gulf, New Orleans, one and the same.

"Hey, guess what, guys," I said to the others who were walking single file ahead of me, sticking close to the buildings to use the iron balconies as shelter. Tip-Top, as usual, was at the lead, hunching her shoulders against the rain's spray. Bigmama studied everything—tourists in their twelve dollar ponchos, pedicabs draped in plastic sheeting. "St. Claude says Grande Red is the dauphine's mother. She's the queen of France."

Elfy stopped so suddenly I almost whammed into her.

"His mother wants to kill him?" she asked.

"Not exactly. She wants him to rule—as does St. Claude—but the dauphine believes claiming the throne in defiance of the new king will lead to his death." I watched Bigmama lean into Tip-Top to pass along the news. Tip-Top inclined her head but otherwise didn't react.

"BTW," I said to Elfy. "You were right about my ditty and the ancient decrees calling Grande Red back. The Duke of Chartres is the one who's taking over the throne in the old king's place."

"His mother is putting him in danger?" she repeated, and I flung my arms around her neck. She didn't give a fig about the political intrigue. All she cared about was a mother violating her sacred duty to keep her babies safe.

"She appears to have very strong opinions," I said as we resumed walking.

"And a too-ready resort to violence," grumbled Elfy whose theory of life must have considered her dead brother-in-law not violence but collateral damage.

At Dumaine we crossed Royal to take cover under a new set of balconies. Tires hissed like a struck match on the wet asphalt. The mist wet my jumpsuit, and it itched against my skin. I raised my cape to shield myself.

The image of the red-caped women with raised knives replayed in my brain. What if Tip-Top had let her knife fly? Or if Bigmama had bonked one of the women on the head with her cudgel, not to mention if Elfy pulled the trigger on her pistol? How would I live if I set such violence in motion . . . again?

I had hoped that by protecting the dauphine, I would redeem the violence I had left in my boss's office. I thought, foolishly, that I might have conjured this entire adventure to give me that redemption. But maybe I couldn't wash violence from my life any more than I could wash away my embarrassingly short arms. Violence and death were genetically sewn into my DNA. Just look at my traveling companions. We were not normal. Like them, my judgment was impaired. Truth was, I might think I was doing right, but I could not be trusted to make the nonviolent choice.

If we managed to find the dauphine and pry him from Grande Red's grasp, I would quit freelancing. I would do exactly what St. Claude asked me to do. I would convince the prince to assume the throne, rule as expected, and not rock the boat. Be normal. Be safe.

Then I would go back to whatever life I could find for myself.

—

My breath caught at the sight of Jackson Square.

Center stage, the cathedral. The cathedral's full name—Cathedral of Saint Louis King of France—said it all, marred only by the statue of ol' Indian killer Andrew Jackson astride his pawing horse. Jackson's name might have been slapped on the square in honor of his leading the Battle of New Orleans, but that was the Americans' doings almost forty years after the battle. The museum exhibits inside the Cabildo told a different story. Post-battle New Orleans was more enthralled with the bravery of the impromptu militia that protected the city—bankers and merchants, Tennessee sharpshooters and Kentucky long-riflemen, Choctaws and seasoned pirates—than they were with Old Hickory or anything American. After all, the American president had told the city he was too busy to help them with the fight. As far as New Orleanians were concerned, the attacking English and the unhelpful Americans were both pretty pathetic.

Given enough time and money, the strong always rewrote history.

Now it was our turn.

Chapter 33

Ignoring the colorful circus of people who always hung out in the square, we edged past Andrew Jackson into the square proper. The iron fountain splished, its music carried by the breeze. I took a deep breath, inhaling the waterlogged river smell. The cathedral, topped by three spires, had a clock in the dead center of its bell tower, which seemed odd to me, more like a life insurance building than a stately cathedral. Over the years, the building had burned and been rebuilt, had rotted from neglect and been refurbished, and received the Pope then re-dubbed a Basilica. Maybe the clock was to get us to focus on the passage of time. Who knows. As if reading my thoughts, the clock chimed eleven. We had arrived at the eleventh hour, the mythical last moment for corrective action before all was lost.

My early days in New Orleans had been wasted. I mean, I spent them literally wasted. Drunk as a skunk curled up at the end of a dark hallway, pressing my cheek against the cool plaster wall in hopes the four Brandy Alexanders I'd slurped wouldn't come hurling back up. When I passed through that phase, I began riding my bike in street clothes on the way to my temp jobs because that was what cool folks in New Orleans did—they rode their bikes for real day-to-day life, not exercise. Saturday nights, I hung out listening to dull jazz at seedy Frenchman Street hideaways or awful bands at the Poland Avenue donut shop that booked bands but only those with food names—The Asphalt Cookies, the Cinnamon Horns, the Space Jammers. Sure, I would never be a full citizen of the city. I hadn't been born here or present in the hours then days then weeks after the canals overflowed and houses began to float. But still I could be hip, not a loser.

Only to arrive in Jackson Square wearing a scratchy red jumpsuit.

The rain, as I predicted, had stopped. Elfy carried the fussing baby, Bigmama sketched the cathedral as she walked, and Tip-Top scraped her wooden shoe across the ground, patrolling up and down our line, protecting us.

A carriage horse shook its neck collar.

A man sang the boom-boom part of "Elvira."

A sketch artist called to passersby, "Draw your likeness?" "Draw your likeness?"

I was here because I was a loser. "Oddly mothered" was the way St. Claude had put it, but it was the same thing. I'd lost in the roulette wheel of life. Drunk parents, grandmothers everyone laughed—or sneered—at. A leg I chose to see as bionic rather than withered, a deformity that in the chain of events had led me to kill my rapist and not even on purpose.

What was I thinking, vowing to be normal? I would never be normal, never be anyone other than me. Sure, I was frightened about calling violence into my life again, but the Bywater had chosen me. I wouldn't shirk that call. Being a loser could be a superpower, right? My superpower. The strong forced violence on others. Us losers saw it coming and punched back. I would take that fact and run with it as far as it would take me. When I reunited with the dauphine, I would support him in whatever path he chose. If violence erupted, so be it. I couldn't stop it anyway. If I thought I could, I was truly living in la-la land.

Did Tip-Top ask to be attacked in two states and have her place of work booby-trapped? Did Elfy beg her husband, please, on your death bed, betray me? Did Bigmama bring the war down on her own head? Did I ask to wind up on the prickly grass, a hand pressed so hard against my mouth I thought my cheekbone would crack?

My grannies and I were born into a violent world, and we fought back. If the willingness to defend ourselves made us abnormal, the problem lay with the world, not us. Shrinking my life to the well-trod path and following the leader, or in this case, the saint, would get me nowhere. In fact, it might get me killed.

If violence was about to strike, I was going down swinging.

Chapter 34

The highest point in Jackson Square was the top floor of the Cabildo, the building to the left of the cathedral. Once the center of government and now a public museum, the Cabildo had a great view. From its paned windows, you could see across the square with its meandering tourists and homeless men sleeping on green benches all the way to the river. Not coincidentally, in the early 1800s, the Cabildo had been the site of the formal ceremony transferring New Orleans from the French to American President Thomas Jefferson. If the dauphine and Grande Red were looking for a vantage point to both view the city and wield their arguments, the third floor of the Cabildo was the ticket.

As Tip-Top passed in her patrol of our small group, I grabbed her arm.

"We need to hit the top floor of that building." I pointed to the Cabildo with its Spanish arched doorways. "An inside staircase on the right takes us upstairs. Don't look at the portraits along the stairs. Actually, don't look at any of the paintings. They'll just make you mad," I advised, remembering the soldiers and the battle scenes with dead, crudely drawn Native Americans tumbled in piles. "On the second floor, a long wide hall runs along the front windows. White curtains on the windows, gold chandeliers, tons of flags, the whole nine yards. At the end of the hall, more stairs up another flight. In the middle of the main room on that floor to the right is Napoleon's mask. I'm betting that's where we find Grande Red and the dauphine. Will you lead us up there?"

Tip-Top tapped the back of my hand. "You and I, we are the same—marked with the brace. But I do not see my intent in you. To lead, you must be ready for the unexpected, and to be ready, you must have intent. What is your intent?"

I stared at her blankly.

She broke off her gaze, blinked at Andrew Jackson, and stared instead at the river.

"Do you know why I walked into the bear trap in the post office that cold morning before the sun was up?"

I shook my head. Was I about to hear the possum story?

"Like I did every day, I entered Hackman's general store and jangled the keys to warn the possum who slept in the grain bin to get his carcass out of my sight. As I wove the aisles to the post office booth at the rear of the store, my lantern cast shadows on the leather saddles and jars of castor oil. I enjoyed the solitude, the ownership of that time. Me, the post office mistress, the one they refused to call ma'am until I controlled their mail. In those hours before the sun rose and Hackman arrived, the store belonged to me. And the possum. Every morning, the possum— he hissed at me, baring his teeth in the lantern light. I did not like him, he did not like me. In that way we got along.

"But the morning I lost my foot, the possum was silent. He was waiting. He had a confederate, you see, one who didn't even know the possum was on his side. The man who held the postmaster position before me was named Bartholomew, Barty, they called him. Barty was fired for opening letters then gumming them back together, and not even doing a good job of it. But Barty believed in himself. He refused to see his own violation of duty had cost him his job. He blamed me. I was the obstacle. If he could only remove me, he would regain his position. Of course, his first step was to spread stories around town about drunken Indians. He counted on my quitting once I felt the hatred rise up against me. He was wrong. So he took it another step."

She was silent for a long minute. Down in the square, pigeons fought over breadcrumbs. "I learned that morning that a possum's hiss and his giggle are different. The giggle is quieter, more personal. I raised my lantern to see why my possum enemy was making that odd snuffling. My eyes were on the animal. I didn't see the trap's open maw. I heard a click then a sharp noise like the pulley-bone on a giant turkey snapping. I stumbled, and glanced down to see my foot slowly flopping over, never to be part of me again."

I wanted to pat her shoulder or something, but like my Tippy, she did not invite touch.

"The townspeople said I was rash, throwing my knife so quickly. But how was I to know the man who rose from behind the coffee bin didn't intend to kill me? I didn't even recognize him as Barty. I saw an evil, looming shadow, and I hurled my knife, intending to kill whoever meant me harm. The town took his side because, after all, he only set the trap to maim, believing a woman with a damaged foot could not stand all day offering the mail. He was almost right. When I resumed my post with the bloody bandage wrapping my nub, the missing foot cried in pain. I too cried out against the lies. The town deemed the man a clever sneak and me a sore loser."

She let a small smile escape. "When the man fell against the grain bin, the possum hissed at me, annoyed at my victory. I did not let him live either."

I wanted to tell her I had really and truly killed by accident. My jutting elbow struck in an instinctive reaction that resulted in unplanned death. But when my boss's fingers glided across my waist, I, like Tip-Top, understood I was in danger. I knew he intended to harm me, and I absolutely intended to prevent that harm from happening. I aimed, I struck. If I had missed, I would have readjusted my aim and jabbed harder. I promise you, my elbow meant to disable the man. I was set on taking him down. I succeeded.

Reading my gaze, she said, "I will lead you up the stairway if you tell me you intend to stop this woman. To protect the dauphine. Whatever it takes, you will not shy away. If you cannot declare that, I will leave you to it."

Leave me?

Like some bizarre marriage vow, I croaked out, "I intend to stop her." Sure, I would try to persuade Grande Red first, but if it went south, I wouldn't wimp out. I wouldn't.

Satisfied, Tip-Top motioned with her head for Bigmama and Elfy to follow us.

To get to the Cabildo, we had to pass through protesters who had converged on the Andrew Jackson statue. They were waving cardboard signs and chanting, "Not his square, our square!" Maneuvering in New Orleans is never easy.

The anti-Jackson protesters had bunched in the path of a group of tourists. Afraid to get separated, the bloc of tourists was advancing on the protesters. The two groups butted up against each other, bouncing in hostility. Tip-Top steered us away from them and led us to a cut-through in the japonica bushes. Inside its branches, we lost sight of the Cabildo's front colonnade.

Plastic soda bottles, chip bags, and a wadded blanket littered our path. Avoiding a charred circle that had probably been somebody's kitchen the night before, I stepped on Elfy's heel, and she stumbled. "Excuse me," I said to her as Bigmama dropped back to make sure we were okay. Tourist talk penetrated the bushes:

"He wanted forty dollars for that piece of shit drawing."

"Has anyone seen Jared since last night?"

"Then the guy says to me, 'You're not from around here, are you?' Apparently, you're supposed to eat beignets with your fingers. So kill me if I like a fork."

Tip-Top, at the head of our line, was already around the curve of the bush. The branches on the bush quivered, and I watched for a flushed bird.

A scarlet-caped woman emerged, knife drawn.

I laughed. Fool me once.

My laugh died. This woman did not have smiling red lips and mascaraed lashes. Her mouth was set in grim determination. Intent, Tip-Top would have said.

The woman raised her knife and pointed it at Elfy and the babe in her arms. My thighs turned cold with sudden, intense shock.

"Run," I rasped.

Chapter 35

At my guttural cry, Bigmama pivoted, whipping out her cudgel. She swung a wide arc and thudded a blow upside the woman's head, dislodging her headcloth and revealing startling white hair. She staggered, almost going down, but recovered and twirled. Scarlet cape billowing, she kicked Bigmama in the gut then glanced around for Elfy and the baby.

I had the baby. Elfy had handed him off to me so she could draw her pistol. I shifted the Hello Kitty knapsack to my back to hide the child and, in a deranged move, crouched with my sword drawn as if preparing to attack. It fooled the minion long enough for Elfy to use her pistol to whack her in the temple. The minion collapsed, splayed in the dirt like a jellyfish.

"It's okay, it's okay," I said, straightening the baby onto my chest. The downed minion's eyes weren't quite shut, revealing pink under-lids. She wore a wooden crucifix, and the gown beneath her cape was seamed with velvet. She looked more like a lady-in-waiting who had fainted than a murderous minion.

Tip-Top squatted beside the unconscious woman, grabbed

her jaw, and wagged her head back and forth. The minion's cheeks flapped like a hound dog.

"Out cold," Tip-Top pronounced.

Bigmama groaned, bending over and wrapping her abdomen. "You might have warned us she was out there." She scowled at Tip-Top. "A fine leader you are."

Tip-Top, who had risen to shake the bushes and make sure no one else was hiding, halted. "Me? You accuse me of being a poor leader? You who trussed us up and led us onto a stage where we were bombed to bits?"

"*I* set you up?" Bigmama squared to face Tip-Top. "My work, my talent—dynamited, it turns out, because the idiot men of the South didn't understand they lost the war."

I wanted to yell at them, but the shock of almost being killed kept words from forming in my brain. I tried to swallow, but my throat was dry as burned toast.

"You deserved to be dynamited." Tip-Top spit on the ground. "Hackman stocked that filth you wrote. 'Leaping Wolf was grateful for a clean bed after his life in the dirty teepee.'"

"It was satire!" Bigmama's voice rose dangerously high.

"Ladies!" Elfy snapped. "Both of you, focus, move forward."

Miraculously, they fell in line, and we double-timed it to the colonnade. As we passed the minion, the baby said, "Nighty, night."

"Shit, shit, shit." I patted the baby on the head to calm him, but I was the one who needed calming. My breath was coming in shallow gulps. Lord Jesus, Elfy could have shot the minion in broad daylight, or Bigmama could have cracked her skull. Big talker me, full of piss and vinegar about random violence, calling it down on our heads.

Bigmama, hands on her hips, twisted as if to stretch out the pain in her abdomen. "Let a horse kick me in the stomach any day. Women."

Tip-Top silently led us around the cannons at the front of the Cabildo, and I glanced down the colonnade to where a single turn would take me to Pirate's Alley. When I first arrived in the city—after I realized the cartoon version of the city waiting in line at Café du Monde and spinning in the Carousel Bar and slurping Hand Grenades on Bourbon was a magician's distraction to keep the real city hidden in the rustling banana leaves—I wandered to the Pirate's Alley bookstore. There I bought a fine leather-bound copy of *The Count of Monte Cristo*, then pulled my hoodie over my head and walked, neck bent, in the rain to Bywater Coffee. Settling in, I drank stiff espresso while I read the twisted tale of the count's revenge. I hadn't cared what anyone thought of me that day, not my soaked jeans or my runny nose. I was in New Orleans reading Dumas in a coffee shop of shared tables while the rain danced bullets on St. Claude Avenue.

The desire to flee welled up in me so strongly, I had to stop myself from running down the colonnade screaming, arms waving, and disappear into the alley. But I couldn't. I had made too many promises—to St. Claude, to the dauphine, to Tip-Top. To the baby, who was batting away my attempts to soothe him.

"We're doing this all for you, buddy," I said, grabbing his hand. "Though your type are notoriously ungrateful. All the dirty diapers and late-night feedings. Thousands of dollars spent on your schooling so you can hate your bougie parents."

He grasped my thumb and stuck it in his mouth. He gummed it, and I had no answer to that.

At the window when the clerk extended her palm and waggled her fingers at me, I shrank back, my palm cupping the baby's head. Whatever my misgivings, I would not hand over the child.

"Cash or credit," she said. "No debit cards."

"Oh, sorry." I dug into my jumper pocket and brought out a wad of twenties. I jiggled the baby as the clerk counted. Seven dollars for the grannies, senior discount; nine for me; baby got in free.

"Ha, ha. Free. That's a joke." I smiled sickly at the clerk.

But Elfy said sweetly, "Don't mind her. The baby's been colicky. Here, give him to me."

She almost ripped the knapsack off my neck.

The walk to the third floor paralyzed me with embarrassment. Never go to the Cabildo with anyone other than a White European. We passed hoards of silver amassed by enslavers using stolen labor, then hit the line drawings of naked Native Americans.

"Oh, look!" I pointed to the display of old-fashioned dresses with tiny waists. "People were so little-bitty back then."

Tip-Top ignored me, steadily rising to the third floor.

Chapter 36

I admit it. I was climbing the stairs, fully expecting to see the dauphine standing at the glass case containing Napoleon's death mask. Or maybe at the window, his back to me as when we had first met. St. Claude had warned me the adult dauphine and the baby dauphine could not lay eyes on each other. Dire consequences would follow, outcomes I deeply did not want.

Yet, had I mentioned the danger to Elfy, the woman who was cuddling the baby against her chest, her eyes alight with love? As she climbed each step, she singsonged, "Oopsie-daisy," and bumped him into the air as if he was on his own personal carnival ride. She had no idea she needed to lag behind. Or even better, turn around and wait for us downstairs. Entertain the baby with the bejeweled harmonica that princes before him had slobbered into. He could play hide-n-seek in the rosewood wardrobe and scare the shit out of the overprotective security guards, or maybe rip the drummer boy's drum off its stand and bang away. Let him tweak the nose of Andrew Jackson's bust or ease him into the wooden pirogue to dream of sliding in and out of guarded bayous with Claiborne's revenuers on his tail. Anything but continue up the stairs.

But Elfy didn't know to alter course. I hadn't told her. I didn't do it on purpose. It slipped my poor, damaged mind.

This is the way it was explained to me by the psychiatrist that, thanks to the trauma of my high school years, I saw at Hinds Community Student Health. Children need protecting. Unfortunately, some children are under the care of adults who can't offer that protection due to drink or drugs or a violent temper or a mindset that wants to instill self-reliance at too young an age. Without the protection they need, those children live in constant fear of the bad thing happening.

Often it does, she assured me, which reinforces the anxiety. Living with constant anxiety causes trauma. Trauma alters the brain. The traumatized brain doesn't function the way it was intended. Instead, it functions in constant panic mode. The confused thinking, the lapses in judgment. The inability to logically think through the consequences of your actions. That's the result: panic mode from trauma, from anxiety, from constant fear from parents who don't protect their kids.

The damage, the tiny gnome-shaped psychiatrist said, slouching in her low-slung chair, could be ameliorated, but never healed. I had a terminal illness. I would die with it onboard.

"You can and should adapt to your limitations." She raised her forefinger. "One, the constant scanning for danger makes you unable to see the forest for the trees. You'll find yourself lost in your surroundings. Carry a map. Two, the panic makes it hard for you to analyze your options on the fly, which means you must step away from a complex situation to vet your next move. Third and final, you'll have trouble holding in your mind anything that has a whiff of danger. No matter how important it is, you will want to expel it from your memory. If something frightens you, you must write it down. You'll think you can retain it, but you can't."

Here she looked at me over her glasses. "Write. It. Down."

But I failed. This morning as I gobbled my eggs and pushed back from the table, I forgot to brush my teeth. I forgot to take my vitamins. And I forgot my notepad and pencil. I clamped on a heavy-ass sword for protection but brought nothing for my damaged brain. When the saint warned me not to let the dauphine and his baby-self lay eyes on each other, my pockets were empty. I did not write it down. I forgot it.

For that, the dauphine paid the price.

Part V

The Meetup

Chapter 37

At the sight of Grande Red and the dauphine standing beside the death mask, relief washed over me. I gulped out a laugh. They were here. I could have been so wrong, stabbing at shit in the dark, spearing a turd. But I was right. We could rescue the dauphine and set him on the path to living his best life.

Beside them, a minion held a tabletop writing desk with a trough for its ink pen and a hole for the inkwell. The minion, whose slit eyes and protruding cheekbones reminded me of women caught up in too much plastic surgery, held the portable desk in her outstretched arms as if offering the sacrament.

Grande Red and the dauphine ignored her. Heads together, they studied a sheet of paper in Grande Red's hands. They seemed so comfortable together, a rush of blood throbbed my temples. Had I misread the whole situation? Was the dauphine actually in cahoots with Grande Red?

No, she was his mother, and even my defective mother— who told me she hadn't taken the morning-after pill because her

AA sponsor thought the responsibility of motherhood would keep her sober—managed moments of intimacy with me. The dauphine was undoubtedly working an angle, hoping to nudge Grande Red to his way of thinking.

Behind them, the third minion gazed out the window, her chubby hands clasped behind her back. She turned and scanned the room, glaring at nothing in particular until she saw us. She was small and piggish, her chin a round ball of clay stuck on her jaw. She wasn't upset to see us. She was happy. She poked out the tip of her tongue, her eyes twinkling with malice. That's what bullies were: baskets of unfocused aggression just looking for a target. Her knife-wielding pal must have seen us from up here and set out to head us off at the pass. She would have killed us to stop the pursuit, maybe harmed the baby too. She failed.

The minion at the window bared her tiny better-to-eat-you-with teeth and squealed, "Mistress."

Grande Red glanced up. Her hair was brick red and fixed in an elaborate updo with braids and twists and turns. Her minions had to be ladies-in-waiting. No way she put that shit together herself. She was tall and thick, and younger than you'd think, but women had kids earlier back then.

"Ah, Etoile, our visioner." The dauphine greeted me with the enthusiasm of a football coach welcoming the star recruit. He was bleary-eyed and smelled of smoke, and I wondered if they had passed the evening in an all-night bar in the lower Quarter. "Good to see you. Let me tell you, I've certainly seen your modern city from the inside out. Down a tunnel." He slid his hand through the air. "Up an arch to nowhere. Spent all night beguiling my mother with my old haunts, but really she was just letting me wear myself out, weren't you, Mother?"

He smiled ingratiatingly at his mom. "Hoping I'd be more malleable when you brought me to the great Napoleon, where my illustrious family history would lead me to sign a decree and meld us all back to our appropriate time period, *n'est-ce pas*?"

When his mother didn't respond, the dauphine waved me

over. "Come, come, Etoile. Meet my lady mother, Queen Princess Maria Theresa of Savoy, Countess of Artois, and wife to Charles X of France."

I stepped forward, my entourage with me, except for Elfy. She had finally made it up the stairs and was showing the baby a sparkly crown that reminded me of the crown on the creepy Burger King dude but was probably worth millions. I think she was removing the baby from the situation, pointing him toward their escape route if all went south. I'm ashamed to say, even that thought failed to remind me of the looming danger.

"My son misspoke. He forgets I am no longer queen, but upon my husband's abdication, Queen Mother to the king." Grande Red inclined her head to the dauphine. Her black lace dress had a flap that ran from her collar to her ankles, similar to what I'd seen nuns wear, but never in lace. Mother-of-pearl earrings curved like scimitars on her ears. I'd kill for those earrings . . . not literally. A huge ruby-encrusted crucifix hung from her neck, and a collection of cameo pins adorned her collar like a five-star general.

"Where is my Gwendolyn?" she asked, the vibrato of her voice the low thrum of water sluicing through a culvert.

"Sleeping it off," Bigmama said, which actually made Tip-Top smile. She and Bigmama had moved in to flank me. In response, the piggish minion inched closer to Grande Red. Earlier, on our way upstairs, a security guard with a body firmly packed into her uniform had asked if we needed help. Bored, undoubtedly. A fine October day, everyone was outside, faces to the sun. The museum was empty. Our group of dead people, and me, were alone.

Both Grande Red and Bigmama were dressed in black, but while Bigmama could have been a Mennonite with her flat front dress, Grande Red was the spitting image of the regal Reverend Mother in Dune (except with hair). Or Snow White's evil queen (but no mirror). Or Cruella de Vil's red-headed Dalmatian-kidnapping cousin, dogless. She was bad ass.

"Gwendolyn attacked us." I plucked at my jumpsuit to let in the cool air—I hadn't noticed how hot it was outside until we stepped into the AC of the Cabildo.

Grande Red looked at me as if I were a slice of old bologna turning green at the back of the fridge. Her gaze traveled over my red jumpsuit, which had begun to sag in the crotch. "The saint's knight. I suppose that's fitting. Claude had one job: to raise a ruler. All those years of teaching, guiding, cajoling. Yet, when the crucial moment arrives, my son wants to voluntarily give up his throne. Voluntarily, I say."

Flashing anger deepened her eyes to violet. The dark circles beneath them were shiny as bruises. They made her look tired and sad, but coupled with her haughty air, regal. I couldn't imagine having her as a mother, but man, I wouldn't mind being her.

"Gwendolyn tried to kill us," I pressed because she hadn't said she was sorry about the attempt on our lives.

Sighing, Grande Red stepped to the side, creating space between herself and the writing-desk minion who tracked her mistress with her gaze. The minion's hard cheeks flamed with rosacea, and her squinty eyes spilled silent tears. Not from sorrow, more like pure distilled frustration. The taffeta beneath Grande Red's lace dress rustled as she shifted, releasing the scent of oranges. A delicate smell for one so stern.

"My ladies are of the highest order, but from time to time Gwendolyn's loyalty leads her to ill-advised aggression." Grande Red refused to acknowledge the fixed stare of her minion, which made me wonder if she had, in fact, ordered the attack and was throwing Gwendolyn under the bus.

I nodded at the sheet of paper in her hand. It had big swirly letters at the top and a signature line at the bottom. It reminded me of Elfy's handiwork.

"What's with the decree?"

Chapter 38

"I never should have trusted Claude de la Colombière," Grande Red said. "He fails, and unable to bear the thought of having his failures unmasked, leaps to distract, hurtling us through time and space. Not backward when we could easily alter events, but forward. The man's sense of direction is atrocious."

"That's gratuitous," I demurred.

"Oh, Mother, for pity's sake." The dauphine slapped his arms against his sides. "The saint and his personal foibles didn't bring us here. The city"—he glanced at me—"and Etoile called us. You—"

His mother spoke over him. "Nevertheless, a good ruler takes the unexpected and snatches it for herself." She raised her hand, and quick as a toad's tongue, snatched an invisible fly from the air. "I will salvage what is in danger of being lost. I will secure the future of our family here in the New World. I will create a new dynasty on new soil."

Her son looked at her with satisfaction. "Lots of *I*'s in that speech, Mother."

She bowed her head, a caricature of the humble servant. I could not imagine many had crossed her, nor her reaction if they did. Her thumb caressed the sheet of paper. "My sole concern, my reason for being on this earth, is you, my son. Though you have hardened your heart against me, I will protect you. For I love you more than I do the heart you have broken."

I saw where the dauphine got his "protest too much" tendencies.

"You label me hard-hearted, Mother, but it is not hard-hearted to disagree with someone. Between Father's utter defeat, your tears, the unspoken threat of being guillotined—in the urgency of the moment, I might have given in and done what you wanted." He straightened. "Thankfully, the city of New Orleans stepped in and brought me here where I had a minute to think."

He spun to face Jackson Square's version of paradise. "The future lies . . . Well, the future lies with the future. Your solution is to resurrect the past. Old things, old ways. That which has been done and done and done again. You want to infect the New World with the old. I want to let it breathe. Look at this beautiful city!"

The queen scoffed. "You cannot attribute the wonders of the future to the Americans. If this coarse, violent country can achieve such a vibrant city, think how much greater it could be under French rule. Under your rule."

"I can wield influence on my own," the dauphine said. "I needn't be king."

"No." She grimaced, and her fist contracted. She might have crumpled her sheet of paper if she hadn't remembered herself. "You never understood the realities of the world. Or perhaps the incompetent Claude did not teach you the most important lesson of history: Deposed rulers face a limited lifespan. The mere presence of a former ruler is a threat to the new ruler. Lurking, waiting to be reinstalled by a disappointed or simply bored people. Soon enough, the new king gives in to his paranoia and whop!"

Her knife-edged palm sliced the air.

The dauphine glanced around the room. "I shall not be a threat, Mother. Perhaps I won't even be in the country."

"*Exactement.*" She moved a step closer to him. "Exile removes the irritation without leaving the stain of bloodshed. But exile isn't sufficient alone. Still the sitting king pitches in his bed. He wakes in a cold sweat. The enemy is at the castle gate, the exiled in tow. Revenge has arrived."

She narrowed her eyes like a huckster pitching the con. "Now, suppose there were a way to dispose of a ruler but remove the threat of return? What circumstances might guarantee a former king no longer wants to return to his former kingdom?"

She threw her hands in the air. "A new kingdom."

"What are you suggesting, Mother?"

"Split the royal line into two kingdoms. One in France, one here in New France. It's simple as child's play."

So, they were arguing, and I was studying Napoleon's death mask. A bronze atrocity that made you imagine the general's cheeks still quivering from his last breath. Molded by French hands, acquired by America as a war trophy or religious relic, I don't know. As far as I was concerned, both countries were indicted.

"Seize this moment," Grande Red urged, her voice rough with passion. "Now, in the interim while you yet hold power. Yes, abdicate, but before you abdicate, use that power to secure the future without exposing your neck to the guillotine. Take the throne and issue a decree creating a new French fiefdom here in New Orleans and keep us in power."

Chapter 39

Wait, what? Preoccupied with Napoleon's morbid death mask, I had missed something. Did Grande Red just suggest France make a fiefdom of New Orleans?

I almost whistled. That was way better than the pitiful theories my group had conjured.

Ask me, it would work. If I'd learned anything on my New Orleans history tour, it was that, while the French citizens of New Orleans weren't happy when the Spanish took over, they hated the Americans. Despised them. Called them uncouth and refused to consent to their rule. There's a reason Canal Street is the widest street in the country: It was the dividing line between the old French sector of the Vieux Carre and the new American sector spreading upriver like a squishy tumor. The French wanted separation. Even the street names of the French Quarter halt abruptly when you hit Canal. The French were like, nope, can't have our street names. Go find your own. 'Cause we *hate* you.

What I'm saying, don't think New Orleans was destined to

be an American city. At the very point the dauphine in France was fighting in the tower with his mother, New Orleans was at its own crossroads. Would the city cry uncle and give in to being American or keep fighting to be French? A move by France to reclaim New Orleans would probably lead the majority of the citizens to break into the Marseillaise. If the French granted the Americans access to the Mississippi River, our government would probably say to NOLA, okay. Y'all be y'all. You're a swampy mess, anyway.

And what a win for Grande Red. I studied her fierce face. It promised bravery and resolute courage. I could easily see her cutting her hair and galloping into battle astride a horse, waving her banner like St. Joan. But she was no Joan. When her husband was forced to abdicate, she did not show courage. She was browbeating her son into doing her work for her. Her mantle of violence hid cowardice, which made me wonder if that was always the case. Violence, which seemed the ultimate strength—maybe it was the ultimate weakness.

If so, what would Grande Red do if the dauphine defied her? If he refused to join in her plan, and she felt the threat of becoming a nobody creeping up behind her, dagger in hand? Not the queen, not Queen Mother. Not even Princess Maria Theresa. Simply Maria. Would she lash out at her son for shredding her dreams? The dauphine said he would die if he ruled, and we were chasing the one who wanted to kill him. Did his mother's fear of losing power leave no room for her son?

A happy giggle echoed against the staircase. The baby dauphine, playing snatch-your-nose with Elfy, who had set him on the floor and squatted down to his level. Elfy had perjured herself to keep her money and shrugged off a man's suicide. Tip-Top had killed because men literally kept trying to trap her. Bigmama had spread a killing lie out of sheer stubborn refusal to admit she had misjudged her audience. Even the softest among us was capable of more than we realized. Would Grande Red sacrifice her child to protect her own power?

"No, Mother." The dauphine interrupted my thoughts. His hand shook as he took the pen his mother offered and slowly set it on the writing desk. "Your scheme won't work. Should I take any official act as king, I seal my fate. If I champion my own cause—any cause—the duke will never accept I don't want his throne. He will lop off my head."

"Son." Grande Red made a fist at her chest, gently tapping her breastbone. "You were born *le fils de France*. You have been respected since you escaped my womb." She shut her eyes. Blue veins danced across her eyelids before she reopened them. "If you give up your throne, you will be a common man, nothing more. No one will value your opinion. They will not even notice your presence. I have lived these humiliations and cannot bear for the indignity to define your future. You don't understand—"

The dauphine held up his palm. "I do understand. You must always be the most clever, the smartest, the one with the best plan—our brilliant Queen Mother. I am merely your irresolute son. Good-natured, a fine hunter, but surely his talents are more suited to the drinking hall than the corridors of power?"

He tried to smile in self-deprecation, but it wobbled. "It doesn't matter. I love you, and I love the family from which I have derived. Being the one who terminates our ruling line, it makes me sick unto death."

The queasy look he'd worn when we first met returned. So that was it. I could see why he might prefer lolling cheap-burgundy-drunk on the rampart to facing this decision. Defying his mother, ending his family's lock on the throne. It couldn't be fun.

"But I have no choice. You steer our family too treacherously. This way and that, wherever your latest scheme takes us, threatening to sink our ship. But this time, all the risk falls on me. If you succeed, you will live out your life as the Queen Mother of a new kingdom. If you fail, you will be the bereaved former queen. Either way, you live. If you are wrong, and I am right, my head is sliced off." He turned to me. "You.

Give me my cape. It's time for me to return home and proceed with abdication."

Startled, I quickly untied the cape. As I swirled it off my shoulders and handed it to him, the baby's head snapped around. He flung himself toward the flaring cape like a bull at a matador.

"Mine! Mine!" he pipped.

Elfy dove for him, but he wiggled from her grasp with the ease of a greased pig.

"Gimme!" he crowed, and his gaze locked on the dauphine.

Chapter 40

When I was in fifth grade, I became obsessed with Bigmama's living room rug. When Elfy ran the vacuum cleaner over the rug in one direction, it was pink as a bunny's nose. When she ran the vacuum back toward her dainty feet, the rug darkened to the deep raspberry in the wineglass my mother held up to the light and said in soft worship, "Nectar of the gods." Fascinated with the transformation, I must have made Elfy run her vacuum back and forth, back and forth a million times.

Later in middle school, pawing through the bottom drawer of the chest in my parent's closet in search of some explanation of who they were, I found a rolled up poster. Snapping off the rubber band, I unrolled the shiny paper and straightened it, arms out. A fish. But as I went to re-roll it, the fish became a lady in a bejeweled gown. I shifted my head. Fish. Lady. Fish. Lady. I was making myself sick. I re-rolled the poster and hid it under my bed.

From time to time, when something I thought was perfect

oozed to shit—a boy I liked targeted me with taunting, my favorite teacher picked on me in class—I unrolled the poster to remind myself that nothing is necessarily what you think it is. Then one night I leaned over the edge of the bed to feel for the poster, but it wasn't there. I snuck back into my parents' closet, and yep, the poster was back in its drawer.

Since then, I'd seen the same phenomenon in the checkerboard pattern of freshly mown lawns—at first, I thought the lawns were dyed or something. Same for oriental rugs running down hotel hallways. Walking to the elevator, dark. Walking toward the lobby, light. Physics books explained it as the direction of the surface and a bending of the light. Neither color was true. Neither was right. What you saw one-hundred percent depended on how you looked at it.

When the man dauphine and the baby dauphine locked eyes, the saint's warning leaped into my brain like a jangling alarm clock.

"Stop!" I yelled and leapt in front of the adult dauphine. I waved my arms, frantic to distract him, make him look at me instead of the baby.

But as I leapt, the man became the baby . . . until I glanced over at Elfy, and the baby became the dauphine. Before I blinked, the man was the baby again.

The same dizziness from the fish-to-lady-to-fish descended, and I staggered. Palms out, I focused on the floor, trying to ground myself.

When I raised my gaze, Grande Red stood alone.

Elfy reached for empty air.

Both the dauphines were gone. In their stead, a teenager smirked.

Chapter 41

"Louis Antoine!"

Grande Red's tone was that of every mother chastising a child who had smeared finger paint on the walls. Except this mother was scolding her son for regressing from a robust adult to a teenage boy.

Elfy spun in circles, her skirt billowing as she lowered herself to the floor. Palms raised, she wailed, "Where did he go? Where is my child?"

Grande Red sneered at her distress. "Who do you call your child? He is not yours. He is mine." She snapped her fingers. A ruby ring on her finger glittered like Dracula. "Louie, come here."

The boy glided toward Elfy who was rubbing her arms as if cold. My Elfy did that whenever she couldn't remember if she had washed the sheets that week. The boy laid his palm on her curved back as if gently knighting her. His brocade jacket was gone. He wore a ruffled white shirt, shirttail out the same way college boys wore button-downs with their wrinkled khakis. He was willowy. I know that sounds girly, but his body curved languidly. He crossed his legs at the ankle. A fish was embroidered on the top of his slipper. A breaching porpoise—no, of course, a rising dolphin.

"I'm too old to need a mother," he said. He wore his nonchalance as if it were new to him, a formal suit he was getting used to. He was well past the age when the world was a mystery to be explained ("Why do earthworms wiggle?") and even past the age when facts spewed like lava ("Did you know squirrels don't like peppermint?" "Did you know ants don't like coffee grounds?"). He had arrived at the point when he was about to drop his childhood loves for new, cooler ones. No telling how being raised as heir to the throne had affected his development. Had he been royally coddled long past his youth? Or had he been expected to mature quickly and stoically? Or both?

"I choose my companions, and I choose her," he said of Elfy, who, under his touch, had risen from the floor. At his mother's scowl, he quickly added, "For today. Maybe tomorrow."

Elfy beamed up at the boy, who was a full head taller than she was. "Have you ever engraved a fork? I saw engraving tools on Napoleon's desk downstairs. Lovely embossed sterling, but sharp. Pointy." She grinned cute as a furry poppet.

Grande Red opened her mouth to make a retort but must have thought better because she spun to the minion with the writing desk. Hurriedly, she scrawled her signature across the bottom of the decree. "You have done me a favor, son. You have returned to your minority. With your father abdicated, I am queen regent. Your protector and legal guardian. The one who can act for you."

She lifted the top of the writing desk to reveal a hidden compartment, slid the decree inside, and slammed the desk shut. Extracting a key from a leather pouch on her belt, she twisted it in the brass lock. The intials MT scrolled across the writing desk's satiny mahogany. She pressed the desk between her palms and handed it to the ghoulish minion. "Guard this with your life, Philiberte."

Turning to her son, Grande Red said, "If you know what is best for you, you will come with me, *Dauphinois.*"

A thoughtful look crossed his face. He fiddled with the hair at the nape of his neck the way I did after a fresh cut. I wondered if he'd only recently had his boyhood locks shorn.

"Perhaps I should tell you," he said, eyes growing wide with determination. At her silence, he straightened as if reciting rehearsed lines. "I will be king, and you will not."

Grande Red flushed with anger, and her breath came quickly. "One day, you'll learn a mother was not made to toy with."

She jerked her head at her minions and strode away, diminished yet somehow even more impressive among us mere mortals. I wanted to call her back, ask her to stay. To show me how to be me, to control my space in this world.

"Etoile," Tip-Top said. "Intent."

"Hey!" I yelled as Grande Red laid her hand on the staircase banister. I wasn't sure what had happened, but I was sure she had forged the dauphine's signature, or signed the decree for him. What mattered, she had told the minion to guard it with her life. Which meant I wanted it. "Come back with that decree!"

I took off running and ran smack into the security guard, who blindsided me in her own mad dash toward our group. I staggered, going down like a bowling pin. She reached out, and I thought she was going to catch me from falling, but she fumbled to grab my arms, her face full of pique. The wannabe cop intended to perp-walk me, and I jerked away.

"If you cain't observe the rules, ya outta here, you and ya fake sword," she grunted, having a go at me again.

"Oh, please." These random jokers needed to help or get out of the way. I moved the sword beyond the reach of her grasping fingers. "The sword's real, by the way. Be careful."

"I'm not playing, gurl," she huffed, her Cajun accent thickening.

"Here, here." Bigmama clapped her hands in the guard's moon pie face and pointed at the staircase. "The woman on the stairs is stealing an exhibit. A Regency period writing desk."

Philiberte paused and glanced over her shoulder. The piggish minion shoved her sister forward, then pivoting, flicked her tongue like a snake scenting a fat white mouse.

She lunged in our direction. The security guard yanked at her gun but forgot the holster was snapped. The butterball minion tackled her, and they rolled on the floor like wrestling inflatables. My money was on the guard, but I couldn't stop to help her. I raced around the pair and descended the stairs in pursuit of Grande Red, who had disappeared.

Chapter 42

My entourage and I skidded into a pile at the foot of the staircase. No Grande Red. No Philiberte with the writing desk. No decree. Just one of those Caution Wet Floor signs with a picture of a man slipping on his keister.

"What the hell?" I exclaimed. "Can't we catch a break?"

Suddenly, Bigmama swiveled and kicked out her lace-up boot in a perfect karate move. The piggish minion was stretched out and flying down the stairs like a bat with fangs. Bigmama's foot caught her full in the stomach.

"Ooof!" The minion dropped and curled into a ball on the stairs, her face contorted in pain. Her scarlet cape twisted around her as if cocooning her into a larva.

"Is she going to liquefy?" I asked.

"She is going to awake with a terrible headache." Tip-Top cocked her head at the downed figure.

"It's always wise to look behind you," Bigmama said. In one quick movement, she hefted the minion over her shoulder, kicked open a closet door, and dumped the beachball inside.

When you wake feeling as if you've been kicked by a mule, you can thank your sister Gwendolyn for that," she said to the prone form. She slammed the door, rattling the mops and brooms.

"Yes!" I pumped my fist in the air. If anyone got in our way, Bigmama would kick 'em and sling 'em and dump 'em in a closet. "Let's go!" I headed toward the exit, eager to chase down Grande Red and retrieve the decree.

Elfy stationed herself between me and the exit, the boy dauphine at her side.

"The dauphine has some questions," she solemnly announced.

He bowed slightly. His skin was as white as St. Claude's except where the saint's was pure as the milk of God, the veins in the dauphine's temples throbbed violet, as if the Creator had let the color seep from his eyes. Though if I nicked that vein with a sharp penknife, I expected no real blood would flow.

"Can you tell me how to book a ship to Paris?" he asked. "I will follow the Mississippi River to the Gulf and cross the sea to France."

"He saw a map upstairs," Elfy said, quivering with pride.

"You want to go back like that?" I pointed up and down his young body.

"Won't work," Bigmama offered. "If we poke him back in time now, he's gonna arrive at this age, not at the age when he left. His mother will pop right back at her current age. She'll arrive in the tower with her forged decree, which will be valid because either he's not there or he's a kid. Our only hope is to stop her before she gets to the castle and travels back to where she came from."

I didn't want to tell Bigmama what I'd seen on the park bridge. Or rather, what I hadn't seen. The castle. Maybe I'd overlooked it. Or maybe it came and went and had reappeared since then. I could not predict the behavior of castles. But despite Bigmama's record so far, I did think she was right about one thing: Surely Grande Red was headed to the castle. If nothing else, we could at least surround her and wrench the decree from her conniving hands.

Bigmama must have seen my uncertainty because she asked, "What?"

"Nothing," I said. "Just a little gas."

As we left the square, we passed Gwendolyn the minion seated on the bumper of an ambulance. She was rubbing the back of her head, and thankfully, didn't see us. Those EMTs were gonna be mighty surprised when they took her blood pressure. Not my problem.

Ol' Indian killer's horse still pawed the air. If Grande Red talked the dauphine into successfully returning New Orleans to the French, the city would not be forced into Washington's tiff with Britain. The Battle of New Orleans would not be fought. The statue would not go up. The square would remain the Place d'Armes, and what would happen with the Civil War was anybody's guess.

Tip-Top touched my arm, asking me to lag behind. I slowed, putting some distance between us and the group.

"I don't want to dash hopes, but when we were on the arch, I did not see the castle. You didn't either, did you?" She stretched her bad leg to the side as if it hurt.

I shook my head, confirming her guess.

"We need an alternate plan in case we arrive, and it isn't there."

"An alternate plan?"

"Intent is not enough, Etoile. As I said, you must have intent and be ready." She unsheathed her bowie knife, and I confess I flinched. She held the blade in front of her face. "This knife was gifted to me by my mother, but it was bought at the post. The knife she used as a child to scrape clinging flesh from deerskin was made by her own hand. If she had wanted, she could have knapped the stone to make me a traditional knife like hers, but that would be foolish. The metal blade is far superior."

She caressed the blade. "Tradition is important but so is functionality. In a White man's world, we needed White man's weapons to be prepared to meet him on his own terms. Are you prepared to meet Grande Red on her terms? What is your plan?"

She waited, and I realized she meant I had to come up with said plan.

I stared at the teenage boy, our new charge. A boy, I'm saying. Who I was supposed to protect.

All three of my grandmothers told and told and told me our family stories. Bigmama told the stories as we circled the garden, and Elfy told the stories as she lunged at dust bunnies hiding under the slipper sofa, and Tippy told the stories as she dipped the needle in alcohol and slid it under my translucent skin, probing for the splinter from the hay barn's rough wood. They steeped me in the stories before I ever learned the first normal rules. ("Don't steal candy." "Always tell the truth." "Make your bed.") I'm sure they believed the world would drill its version of right and wrong into my soft skull soon enough, but the lessons of the stories couldn't wait.

What was the lesson? There was something fundamentally wrong in this world. Not with men. With the society men had constructed. The moral: Society doesn't work for women. Period. Don't expect it to, and you won't be disappointed. Expect equality and fair play, and you will wind up disinherited, belittled, and jailed for protecting yourself from rape.

I had believed my grannies' stories protected me. I thought they kept me from being fooled by the rules that favored those who made the rules. (Why do you think hotheaded crimes of passion are forgiven, but woman-favored murder for hire is punished more severely than murder?) The lessons had become real when I stared at the glittery obelisk embedded between my boss's shoulder blades. Karma, dude.

Now this heretical view—refuse to trust the rules of society—was being called upon to protect not women but the young man by Elfy's side, as Tip-Top waited for me to come up with a genius plan.

God only knows where it would lead.

Part VI

A New Type of Hunt

Chapter 43

Our group milled on the sidewalk, dispirited. On the way to the castle, we had explained our errand to the dauphine. He was shocked to hear that his father had been forced to abdicate, but he was a flexible boy, quick to accept the nonsense of his current situation. He immediately became excited about leaving New Orleans via castle. I liked him. To be honest, I had liked all three versions of him. The adult dauphine was empathetic and earnest. The baby was adorable and spunky. This teenage dauphine was endearing in his striving to be adult while breaking into puppyish enthusiasm. I didn't know why St. Claude had said I would want the dauphine to die. I simply couldn't imagine it.

When we arrived, the castle wasn't where we'd left it.

Who knows whether the house now on the lot was there before the castle appeared. It was a new house, post-Katrina and, unlike most of those in the Bywater, hadn't been built to pretend it was pre-storm. I had a sudden thought the house might be like the Tardis: yellow and gray house on the outside, castle on the inside. Wading through the cast iron plants, I cupped my hands and peered in the window. Mid-century modern, no suits of armor.

My grannies were having a conversation among themselves, but the boy pivoted to his original plan. "She returns to Paris. We must head to the docks."

He swung his arms in the direction of the river.

"This isn't a nineteenth century pirate novel," I told him, but not unkindly. "Your mom can't stow away. They won't allow her on a ship without a passport and a ticket, which means money plus a reservation. How would she even know which ship to take?"

The young man adjusted his cape, spreading it wide to study its gold-star lining. "Mother never acts alone. However long she's been in this city, she will have been developing contacts. Seeding money. Finding those willing to help her. She will create cohorts, and she will use them."

His statement set off a buzzing in my brain like when I'd forgotten I'd taken an Aleve and took another. Grande Red already had a contact in the city.

I threw back my head. "St. Claude! Come down here right this minute!"

Silence.

"Claude, I know you're out there. You're listening to everything." Then I remembered he actually didn't hear my talking. *You better get your old-saint ass down here right now, or I'm gonna tell your prize student all about you and the nun. The close quarters. The long lessons. The almost-touching knees. The—*

"Threats unbecome you, Etoile."

The saint's voice came from overhead. He was perched in the vee of a crepe myrtle. Russet leaves fluttered around him. With his robe hanging down, he looked like a girl playing ghost.

"Claude. Can you come a little closer?"

He stuffed a wedge of cake into his mouth and licked—oh,

my lord—purple and green icing from his fingers. Above his head, an exposed bird nest circled like a halo.

"You know it's bad luck to eat king cake out of season, right?" I said, trying to josh him out of the tree. "We're all gonna die, thanks to that sacrilege."

His grip on the peeling bark of the crepe myrtle tightened. He had caught sight of the teenage dauphine. Down the street, earthmoving equipment rumbled. It was 2018, thirteen years after the storm, but the frenzy of repairs set off by Katrina's Road Home money continued. They were laying a new streetcar line on St. Claude (the avenue, not the man). The air was drenched with an earthen smell, and culverts big as hobbit homes lay on the neutral ground awaiting burial.

"Etoile?"

"Yes, Claude?"

"Did you ignore my warning about the dauphines meeting?"

"No," I said, because technically ignoring required remembering, and I had totally forgotten. "Did Grande Red come here? Have you been helping her?"

His lips worked like an inchworm moving forward—small contracting movements with not much progress. His flushed skin put me in mind of the rosy scalp peeking through the fur of the white mice we kept in cages in elementary school to teach us to care for another living thing. Innocent, they looked. But one of those mice, when I tried to feed it, drew blood.

A terrible thought occurred to me. "Did Grande Red come running here, and you whooshed her away in the castle?"

"I do not whoosh," he said with great umbrage.

"Then tell me where the castle went, Claude. How do these people return to their time if the castle is gone?"

"And what is their time, Etoile?" he asked, lifting a palm. "Is it when this young man was on the cusp of ruling and all our efforts were bent toward preparing him for the responsibilities to come? Or is it the time of the baby you last had in your possession—when French power in the world was contracting thanks to the megalomaniac Bonaparte—and the desire for a true, righteous king was rekindled? Or is it the moment when the adult dauphine declared to his mother he would decline the throne despite the vow of our rival house to tear down all that was civilized and leave a decimated Church bobbing in its wake? When is 'their time,' Etoile?"

His face was blotched red with fury, his lips bloodless. He looked as if he wanted to throttle me. I suppose I should have been cowed. For all I knew, he could upchuck fireballs. But that was the benefit of being raised by women. Male fury did not impress. I hadn't grown up swimming in that slimy sea, so I recognized it for what it was: an impotent lion roaring to intimidate. Pitiful, but also dangerous. Fail to bow down, and the lion might charge.

Elfy touched my arm.

And there it was. What I'd been waiting for all those years after Bigmama and Elfy died, and Tippy was sliding into dementia on the farm, and I was making a disastrous job choice. The touch that told me someone had my back.

"May I?" she asked.

I gratefully stepped aside.

"Monsieur Claude, did I hear you say something about fearing the decimation of the Church?" Elfy neared the saint's tree, signaling to the rest of us to stay put. She moved as if she took up more space than she did, maybe anticipating her future plumpness. She fluffed her hair, prepping.

"Are you facing a threat to something you love dearly?" she asked the saint, her voice as understanding as a snake charmer. In response, the saint's pointy head ticktocked from side to side.

"If those who would rule in place of the dauphine were a danger to your Church, I can see why you would be upset. Shame on them." She tsked as the saint gradually descended the tree to stand beside her.

She slipped her arm in Claude's and fingered the stiff lace cuff of his sleeve.

"You're a clever man, Claude. I'm sure you have an alternative plan should it turn out that none of this," she circled her hand in the air, "works out. If, despite your attempts to send us hither and yon, despite your persuasive powers, despite the mountains you've moved to get him to take the throne, what if the dauphine chooses not to rule? If that happened, what would be your clever solution to ensure the future of your Church under the new regime?"

She turned her face up to him. With her large green eyes, black curls, creamy white skin, and red lips, she was a caricature of a Scarlett O'Hara Southern belle.

The saint tucked his chin to look down at her. "I do believe the answer lies—"

Elfy held up her small palm. "Forgive me, but I suspect your plans are too complicated for my tiny woman's brain to absorb. Or maybe it is really very simple. Perhaps you plan to assassinate your rival? That would be the simplest, would it not? Let the dauphine do as he wishes—rule, not rule—and take care of the problem yourself? You could leave the dauphine out of this entirely, couldn't you . . . if you had but the courage of your convictions?"

She smiled sweetly at him, her eyes full of venom.

Chapter 44

The saint's pride, which had puffed under Elfy's flattery, melted. He must have decided her suggestion of assassination couldn't be serious, because amusement took over.

"Mademoiselle, I believe Etoile is lucky to have you on—"

"Madam," Elfy corrected him. "You supported Grande Red because she told you she would guarantee her son's protection of your Church. Of course, you expected she would fulfill that promise by settling him on the French throne. Was there any other? I'm thinking she showed up here with her signed decree and plan to place him on a New Orleans throne. You realized, if the intent was for the dauphine to rule from this land, y'all no longer needed him to return to France. You tell yourself, hey, he loves New Orleans, but the truth is, he's never been anything more than a tool for you and his mother. So you pointed Grande Red the way home."

Claude cleared his throat. Behind him, a black cat picked its way around the broken glass protecting the top of a courtyard wall. "As you say, the most important concern is the Mother Church, and Grande Red is its most able defender. But." He glanced nervously at the slanting roof of the house that had replaced the now-missing castle.

"Ah." Elfy tapped his forearm. "Excuse me."

She returned to our group, which had been watching her performance. She spoke as if the saint couldn't hear her, which of course he could.

"He would have sold the boy down the river, but the castle wouldn't cooperate. Who knew castles had consciences?" She gazed down the street. "Anyway, the castle retreated. Grande Red must find her own way home. As to us, we must find the castle so the dauphine can return home to make his own choices."

The saint waved both hands at Elfy as if to ward off her words. "You don't understand. It does no good to resummon the castle, not with the dauphine like this." He flicked his wrist at the teenage dauphine. "This boy cannot make the adult dauphine's decision. Nor does Grande Red need him. She can return with her signed decree to the moment in the tower and implement it. She believes she has achieved the best of both worlds. The power of a throne she desires, albeit in the new kingdom, and her son still a minor she can control."

"But what?" I asked because there was a loud "but" at the end of that explanation.

"When she implements the decree and alters the timeline, any . . . iteration of the prince remaining on this side of time will be as a wart tied with a string."

"A wart? The dauphine is a wart?" I was horrified. Surely the saint didn't want to subject the dauphine to the same treatment my Tippy had used on my warty finger: Tie a string around it, cut off the blood supply. "He dies and drops off?"

"That is the outcome, yes." The saint nibbled a hangnail then hid his hand behind his flowing robe.

"But then her plan fails. No dauphine, no New France, no

power-proud Grande Red."

The saint took on the ashamed look of the stray cur that hung out around Tippy's back door, as if you had caught him eating his own vomit.

"You didn't tell her? She doesn't know she must grow him up before she returns?" I asked, incredulous. "Oh, wait. An adult dauphine making his own decisions doesn't suit y'all's plans, does it? You want him to solve your problems for you, but heaven forbid you look out for his safety. Men," I added in disgust.

His embarrassment slid away, replaced by anger. "You believe me capable of that? I wanted the young man on the throne in France. Not simply to protect the Church—the throne is where he would be safest. But before I could explain the situation, the Queen Mother fled during the chaos of the retreating castle. I would never have sentenced the poor boy to this fate, and I question your judgment if you believe I would."

"I stand beside you, hearing every word you say," the dauphine pondered.

"I am of the opinion—" Claude began.

"Did it ever occur to you that your opinion isn't the one that counts here? I was called by the Bywater." I stabbed my chest with my thumb. "I called forth my grannies. I am the hero. You know why you're here? Because it's the name of a street. It's not St. Vincent Avenue. Or St. Bart. Or St. Kit." My brain was stuck on Caribbean islands, and I shook my head to clear it. "The street is St. Claude Avenue. And that's the only reason you're here."

"I would never willingly betray this young man." He ticked his head toward the young dauphine who, following the "wart" remark, Tip-Top and Bigmama had flanked in a protective maneuver. "He has been my life's work. His mother, God bless her, is a magnificent but strong-willed woman. She does have her blindside when it comes to her sisters, who are vindictive, cruel women with hearts black as a chicken's tongue. They misled her—"

I interrupted his tiny-violin playing. "You told her the secret to getting home, didn't you? What was it? Tap your heels and repeat three times, 'I do believe in ghosts, I do believe in ghosts'? Or is it some super-secret church handshake?"

Had he even wanted me to get the dauphine off the rampart? Or had he hoped I'd go up there and harangue the poor boy about ruling until he pitched himself onto the sidewalk? The dauphine had suspected someone wanted him to stay on the rampart drunk. Maybe it had been St. Claude himself.

It made me so mad I could spit nails. Betrayed by a saint! And one I really, really liked. People were such selfish shits, caring about nobody but themselves. Thank you Jesus the castle was on my side. But fat lot of good that did me.

I needed to calm down.

"The castle is the way home, Etoile." Claude rubbed his neck as if I'd been holding him in a chokehold. "There is no secret way. I would have told the insistent Sister Philiberte as much if she had but given me a chance."

"Sister?" I repeated. He had used that word twice to describe the minions. "She's not a sis-ter. She's Whiter than I am."

"A sister," Elfy said to me softly. "A cloistered woman. A nun."

"They're nuns?" The gears in my brain whirled. Claude trusting Grande Red to protect his Church. The two of them conspiring over their love of the Church. Her black dress like a nun's. Her big-ass crucifix.

"She's your nun?" I gawped at the saint.

"What do you mean, my nun?" Claude drew back. "Why do you keep making such insinuations?"

"You and the nun at your monastery in Burgundy. The cloister attached to it with the tiny changing room." I explained the little I knew about him and the nun. "You were her confessor. You got all cozy. Good friends. Spiritual companions. You exited this world a doddering old man in love with a nun who had visions."

Claude looked like he'd swallowed a frog. "This is something you know will come true?"

"Let's just say I'm putting two and two together, and I'm not getting five."

I turned to Elfy. "And you suspected."

"The flame of love burns brightest at its kindling. 'Tis easy to see," she said, as if I was a simpleton.

"Oh, dear me." Claude waned. I mean, he literally began to fade.

"Hey—no fair!" I jumped up and down. "Come back here! Tell me what to do."

But I was yelling at a bare crepe myrtle on an empty sidewalk.

"Grande Red will trick the castle," Bigmama said into the silence. "Pretend she's changed her mind. Tell the castle she wants to go home to see if her son is waiting for her."

"Shhhh." Tip-Top held a finger to her lips. "He must figure it out."

"Who?" I asked. "That wimp of a saint isn't coming back."

"No. Him."

We all turned to the teenage dauphine.

Chapter 45

You caught St. Claude's reaction to the Grande Red news, right? He wasn't protesting, trying to hide the truth. The saint was totally surprised about him and the nun. He had no clue. St. Claude being dead, he should have known the totality of his life. Either these folks traipsing around New Orleans in French court getup weren't who they claimed to be, or something was off about the timeline. It was like the time when I'd been getting ready for a party, and a vintage necklace I'd been clasping around my neck broke. Fake pearls cascaded to the floor. In my hand hung what had formed these random pieces into a necklace: a limp, dirty string.

Who knows what actually holds the universe together.

—

"You heard what the old man said." Tip-Top looked at the empty spot where the saint had stood. "The boy must grow up, and quickly."

She stuck out her good foot, what I had come to see as her

aggressive stance. I wished I'd known that trick when I was growing up. "Put your best foot forward," everyone said, but Tip-Top actually did it. Her foot rested on the blue and white tiles embedded in the concrete and proclaiming the street to be Montegut. No similar tiles told you we were on the corner of St. Claude and Montegut, which is why I had been forced to make up the ditty that rocketed us into this adventure.

The word *intent* floated into my brain, and I tried to focus, but it was becoming harder and harder. I concentrated on the teenage dauphine, the subject at hand.

"Grow a man from the boy?" Elfy offered the teenage dauphine a mischievous smile that dimpled her cheeks. "That's easy. We send him to Bourbon Street."

Well. Elfy the professional seductress actually did know the city, or at least the street notorious for strip joints and S-E-X.

"No," I said before the others could get into an argument. "We aren't going the sex route, or the violence route, either, if anyone's thinking about proposing that one."

"Don't look at me." Bigmama held up her palms. "I had the one daughter." Under her breath she added, "Thank you, Jesus." Which reminded me, again, that we were, each one, shit for this quest.

"I already told you," Tip-Top said, slightly exasperated. "Mastery of a task is what grows us up. Male, female, it makes no difference. The task has been given to him, which makes it so simple not even you women can mess it up. He must find his mother."

"Do you agree?" I turned to the dauphine. "Does the idea of successfully tracking down your mom and deciding how to handle the situation when we find her generate a sense of accomplishment in you? Does the thought of succeeding make you feel more mature?"

If so, the dauphine was going to learn this lesson way easier than my boss had. As the man had sat ragdoll against the wall, I leaned over him, my nose so close to the blood pooling on the carpet, I fancied I could smell the cheap garlic toast he ate every lunchtime at the corner diner. I whispered in his ear, "You're on your own now, Donald." He groaned, a short expulsion of breath, maybe his last. Who knows? But I stuck to my guns and left. The man had receptionists and secretaries and female underlings and a stay-at-home doting wife. How would he ever learn to stand on his own two feet if we kept bailing him out?

The dauphine nodded, completely solemn. "I agree."

"Okay. It's settled." I clapped my hands in one sharp crack, like a Saturday morning "get 'er done" cartoon. "Where to, dauphine?"

"My name is Louis." He bowed to me, extending his arm in a flourish. "I am the dauphine, but in address, I am Louis Antoine, Duke of Angouleme. Or, because you are friends who hope to save my life, Louie. We must seek French sympathizers. A place *ma mère* has encountered recently. How long has she been in your fair city?"

"Since yesterday afternoon," I told him. "So, almost twenty-four hours?"

"Very well. We must divide her time into quadrants. Afternoon. Evening. Night. Morning." He air-chopped his arm into four equal sections. "What afternoon venues, what evening venues, and so on would attract those who remain loyal to France?"

I had been really impressed with his logical thinking until that last part. Then it dawned on me he didn't know how much time had passed since anyone in New Orleans had been loyal to France. "Dauphine . . . Louie. You need to know. The year is 2018."

"*Pas possible!*" he exclaimed.

I didn't know how to make it any easier on him, and I wasn't sure that was the point of this exercise. I turned to Tip-Top for guidance on her idea. "How much help can we give him?"

She shrugged. "As much as any parent helps a child while still allowing for independence."

I stared at her, eyebrows raised, waiting for her to realize she had fallen into that universal trap of assuming every human being on the planet had procreated.

"Ask questions," Bigmama offered.

"Okay." I returned my attention to the dauphine. "What would your mother be attracted to? Like, for example, what did she make a beeline to inside the Cabildo?" I waggled my brows to reinforce the hint.

"That is not allowing for independence," Tip-Top observed, but the dauphine looked puzzled.

"Right," I said. "You weren't there—at least, this you wasn't. I'll give you information, and you sort it."

I assumed a stance as if I were an oracle: legs spread, palms up, wrists cocked at an angle.

"As best we know, your mother went to a high arch by the river here in the neighborhood to survey the city." I swept my hands in an arc. "She discovered a tunnel that led to a pop-up shop." I dug the tunnel with my hands then popped up. "She lured the adult you into the shop, smuggled you/him down the tunnel, then accompanied y'all in a nighttime review of your old haunts in the city. The next morning"—I pantomimed the sun rising—"her first act was to go straight to the Cabildo to find Napoleon's death mask."

"She will seek out another Napoleonic place," Louis said immediately.

"Bingo!" I cried. "To the Napoleon House, it is."

At their blank stares, I added, "The Napoleon House. It's a restaurant in the Quarter."

I thought we had done pretty well as a team, but Tip-Top and Elfy both glared at me, and maybe I had led the boy a bit. So what? As long as he thought he was in charge, he would assume himself astoundingly accomplished. After all, wasn't that the way women had been dealing with men since time immemorial—protect their notorious egos, and get 'er done?

Chapter 46

As our krewe proceeded toward the French Quarter, a cluster of birds swerved overhead. Birds were always swerving over New Orleans. I guess they were headed to the Gulf of Mexico, but who's to say I knew anything at all about this city, or what we were doing, or who I was with.

"Boy, that St. Claude is a disappointment," I said to Bigmama. "He's practically a traitor, and I thought he was the Bywater representative. You know, like a Ninth Ward rep on the city council, only dead."

"You thought he represented the neighborhood because he told you he did. But we all lie. Or shade. Or omit. The effect is the same." Bigmama paused to examine a white fleur-de-lis on a black garbage can. It was a striking work of art, on city trash cans. The house it sat in front of looked abandoned, with peeled paint, mossy steps, and rusted fencing, but the garbage can overflowed. Never make assumptions about what was alive in New Orleans.

"I liked him," I said.

"He intended for you to like him."

So easy to confuse how you felt about someone with how they felt about you.

Then she added, "And he may come back around to our side, you never know. Don't burn your bridges. Always give a person room to surprise you. With a little cajoling, anything is possible."

Her and her poison pen, her idea of cajoling was a bit different from mine, but I said nothing.

Up front, Louie had halted. He was gesturing heatedly, Elfy and Tip-Top looking down the side street where he pointed. He was clearly excited about something.

"*C'est la*," he said as we approached. I read the sign: Frenchmen Street.

"Ya think?" I asked. If we followed every French lead the city offered, we'd be running around like chickens with our heads cut off.

"If one were looking for those loyal to France, would one not look on Frenchman Street?" he posited.

If one did, one probably would be disappointed. But I could be wrong. The street was named for a group of French loyalists who took up arms at the thought of New Orleans being ceded to Spain, for which they were executed. If New Orleans had been infected by the weird reality of our group, and French loyalists were lurking, they might very well be on Frenchmen Street. Besides, we had to cut to the river sooner or later, and Frenchmen Street was as good a route as any.

"It's your call," I said and dropped back so he could make it.

His gaze tracked me and then shifted to Elfy. Early on, I'd gotten the impression he believed Elfy was our leader. Then, gradually, the more I talked, he came to view me as the head knocker of the group. Yet, he was clearly attached to Elfy, and like a gosling to its mama, turned instinctively to her for support.

Now, she worked to keep her face neutral.

The peculiar vein in the dauphine's temple throbbed, its pale violet the color of the wine stain on the shell of an oyster, the purest of bivalves.

"We reconnoiter the street," he said, leading the way across St. Claude toward Frenchmen. We navigated the streetcar tracks, stepping carefully. For a moment, I thought a woman dragging a little girl by the hand was flagging us down, but she was running for the streetcar, waving at the conductor while the pale faces of the passengers observed her distress.

I hurried to catch up with the group. A sheet of paper swirled in the breeze and attached itself to my leg. I pried it loose and shook it free, setting it on its way. I feared Louie was making an amateur mistake—take the opposite position of those around you and call it independence, but as I said, no harm could come of it. Frenchmen led us to the French Quarter, which was where we wanted to go.

Only later did I remember that old saying about the journey being the point, which meant a rocky journey could be an utter failure.

—

We lost the dauphine.

I know, I know. But late afternoon was arriving, and the music scene on Frenchman Street was tuning up. The alley beside the Spotted Cat was alive with tourists. Music seeped from every restaurant and bar, a symphony of guitars and horns and somewhere a fiddle. The lights outside the Blue Nile had kicked on, and the whole sidewalk was awash in royal blue. Elfy stopped to admire the effect. Then Bigmama, and finally Tip-Top, as if they were succumbing to poppies in the field. Even I paused to gaze at the glory of the street. It was really something to a chick whose parents drank Bloody Marys at night on an oil-stained carport while I coiled in my molded plastic chair like a knot of barbed wire. Picking the pine straw out of my Kool-Aid, hoping my parents would keep laughing at the sparklers catching the leggy azaleas on fire, giving me a happy Fourth of July by making an effort at parenting. Better than Mom clicking off the blender at ten o'clock in the morning so she could hiss at me, "You will not shame me." But apparently I did that just by breathing the same air. On Frenchmen Street, they were sophisticated. They did not drink Bloody Marys at night. I turned to nudge Louie onward, but my elbow hit thin air.

I tapped Tip-Top, who tapped Bigmama who asked Elfy, "Where's your boy?"

Elfy widened her eyes and then threw back her head and called, "Dauphine! Where are you?"

"Y'all looking for a boy in a cape?" A skinny Black man with cigarette breath pressed his fingers into my forearm. "That him, sneaking into the Cat?"

I looked up just in time to see Louie's cape fluttering through the door of the club.

I waded through the crowd bunched at the Cat's front door and shouldered past the bouncer—hell if I'd pay a cover just to fetch Louie out of there. As I passed, sword clanging, someone in the group yelled, "Make way for Monte Python!" I saw the dauphine immediately. He was on the postage stamp sized stage with the standing mic angled toward him, Elvis style. He was singing the Marseillaise. The audience was rising to its feet like a deranged *Casablanca*.

I cupped my hands to form a megaphone and hollered, "Hey, Louie!"

This caused the band to segue into "Louie, Louie," and the audience to sway drunkenly to the chorus. Right as the lyrics announced the intent to go, Louie did go. He stomped off the stage. I grabbed his forearm and led him through the throng of people to the blessed fresh air.

Louie brushed himself off.

I leaned in and sniffed. Beer.

"The people were shouting about being in the right place at the wrong time," he said. "I felt it to be a sign, as nothing more adequately describes my situation at this moment. Right place, wrong time?"

He opened his palms in a one-or-the-other gesture, and I realized the boy relied on extravagant hand motions. Had the adult dauphine done that? If not, what made him grow out of the affectation?

The boy's arms serpentined as he shifted to explain his actions to Bigmama, his fingers splayed like a lady's fan. With the cape as a backdrop, it put me in mind of a magician. He wasn't as beautiful as he would grow to be, but he was lovely enough that his weaving arms seemed to practice seduction. The adult dauphine had done that when we first met, cast his spell over me and the grannies. I had thought he was unaware of his effect, but it was hard to analyze someone when your brain was preoccupied with the impression you were making on the gorgeous creature in front of you.

"His arms reveal a secretiveness, don't you think?" Tip-Top asked. She mimicked his motions in small movements, as if that would help her understand. The shining sun turned her hair to black lava. "Much like the older dauphine, who beguiled us into accepting his version of the situation at the castle."

"But it stopped. When?" I cast back. The dauphine's full-bore attention to us had abruptly ended when he asked us to help him find his nemesis. Had that been his goal, to get us to leave the castle with him?

"You think he manipulated us into this quest?" I asked.

"I think it is an asset the boy uses to gain dominance. He focused first on Mrs. Morris, singling her out as his substitute mother, right in front of his own mother," Tip-Top said. "Now that she is securely in hand, he turns his attention to Mrs. Daniels. I suspect I will be next. He'll save you for last to make sure he has a crowd behind him before he tackles the leader."

Louie released a smidgen of a smile toward me and Tip-Top, and I wondered if he were a dangerous, silly boy.

The grannies gathered around him. Above their heads, the

Spotted Cat's wooden sign of a cat playing a sax swung in time with the thumping music. They began to advise him. Elfy warned him about the attention of ladies. Bigmama asked him to imagine a successful mission and follow that thread. Tip-Top mumbled something about how to outwit a stoplight. Only later did I realize the conversation full of wisdom and concern was the guarantee our mission would fail.

Chapter 47

We followed Chartres Street toward the French Quarter without speaking. Tip-Top breathed heavily. Elfy glanced at her reflection in an antique store window and smoothed an eyebrow. We passed a clique of brightly colored ducks waddling down the neutral ground on Esplanade, and Bigmama retrieved her journal from her sash. I concentrated on my step. The Marigny, land of cracked sidewalks, was a son of a bitch to navigate with a brace on your foot.

As we galumphed under a balcony and out the other side, I considered the irony of our quest. We four women were trying to teach the dauphine to do what none of us had done: take responsibility for one's life. For all the family history passed down to me, for everything the women walking beside me had lived through and accomplished, the heartbreak and joy, the crime and justice—not one of us had owned up publicly to our failings. And by failings, I mean killings.

Sure, Tip-Top's last two killings had been forced into the light when she had been charged and had to argue self-defense, but the first Alabama killing she kept in the shadows. Elfy never admitted—much less apologized for—manipulating her brother-in-law to the point of suicide. Bigmama railed against the stupidity of her readers, but never recanted her parodies of the obscene Old South. When the people lapped up her stories like cats after cream, she doubled down. When each greater cartoonish exaggeration failed to knock her readers awake, she blamed them, not her pen. At least that was what Elfy told me the day her anger erupted at Bigmama for hijacking our cleaning time. "Just as selfish as her ancestor," she fumed, "except her ancestor had the blood of thousands on her hands." She tightened the belt on her flowered dress and worked her jaw, chewing on what wasn't there. That was nothing compared to what Bigmama told me about the first Elfy.

A Gay Pride flag flapped in the ever-present breeze. My foot ached from the walking, and I reached to adjust the brace. Technically, I wasn't a fugitive from the law. The law had decided my boss's death was a freak accident. Which it was. But I hadn't stepped forward to describe the chain of events that led to the accident. ("Why did you react so violently to a mere elbow brush? Oh, he raped you? So you had reason to want him impaled on an obelisk?") Hell if I'd expose myself to a system I'd been taught since birth did not work in my favor. Said me. Said Tip-Top Said Elfy. Said Bigmama.

The dauphine hummed a tune. When he broke into words, he had the same lovely voice as his adult self. Odd hearing him sing Dr. John, but what wasn't odd? If all went as planned, the dauphine would lead us to Grande Red. He would persuade her to hand over the decree, and we would trot off to the resurrected castle with the grown-up dauphine who would return to France to live the life he chose. He had male confidence, but would the royal system allow him his choice?

He hurried ahead to ask Elfy something. Her face radiated toward him like a flower finding the sun. Could he live as a private citizen if that's what he wanted? Or would the system squelch him as soon as he stepped out of the royal line?

"A penny for your thoughts," Bigmama said at my side.

"Look at that." I gestured to a window wrapped in purple, green, and gold shimmery bunting. "The French Quarter always has to be like, 'It's Mardi Gras!' even if it's October. Give it a rest, for Pete's sake."

"Other than objecting to the decorations?" Bigmama asked.

"Systems suck," I said. "They don't care about the person. They want what they want, and if they have to kill everyone in their path to get it, that's fine too."

Bigmama was quiet for a moment. Ahead of us, the moon was visible in the sky alongside the waning sun, low on the horizon and milky white, not yet its time of the month.

"Is there something you'd like to tell me?" she asked. Just like my own Bigmama when she discovered me huddled in the bathtub after punching that Prather boy in the nose for calling my mother a drunk.

A bicycle gained on us, bell dinging its approach, gold tinsel fluttering. The Godzilla bike I'd seen earlier. When all this was over, I was getting me a bike like that. I stepped closer to Bigmama for it to wedge past, but it veered into the street at the last minute.

"I have this long hallway." I paralleled my arms in front of me, demonstrating the hall. "It's sectioned by firewalls, you know, those heavy doors that provide the last defense against a raging fire. Over time, I pass from section to section, and as I pass through a section, I shut the door behind me." I slammed the imaginary door. "If a fire breaks out in one of the dead sections"—I imagined Tippy after she became demented stabbing herself with a nail file or Mother furiously clicking off the blender or Bigmama and Elfy sparring over my companionship—"the firewall will contain it. I'll be safe. But this NOLA section is mixing all the sections together like lemon in milk, curdling my life."

"Is there something more concrete you want to tell me?" she

pressed, her voice patient.

I looked straight at her. "I killed a man. My boss. I impaled him and left him to die."

Chapter 48

I could feel Bigmama assessing me, but I stared straight ahead. Soon we would pass through Jackson Square again, back at the cathedral. We walked through the yellow sunlight that signaled the coming end of an October day. I drank in the heavy smell of confectioners' sugar drifting from Café du Monde where tourists walked away with full bellies and napkins stuck to their shoes. I didn't want to defend myself or fight with Bigmama. I hadn't in real life with my own Bigmama, and starting now with my dead ancestor seemed ridiculous. But I never followed my own good advice.

"You want me to be a badass like you. Tell myself, yeah, I killed him. He deserved it. But you don't know what it's like to carry guilt." I shoved my bangs aside—I wouldn't be the type of chicken shit who wouldn't look at her when I accused her. "Sure, you brandished words like a razor, but that's a metaphor. Actually, killing is different."

Anguish filled her eyes. "Oh, Etoile."

It hit me.

"I'm wrong. You did kill someone."

"I didn't kill *someone*."

"Oh." I pictured baby Jewel poking her thumb in the cannonball divot in her parlor.

Bigmama straightened her shoulders, as if giving herself courage. Her voice cracked when she began. It almost broke my heart, her being vulnerable.

"I was alone, cut off. My father-in-law had been lost to the sword, my brother dying by the bloody flux. I hadn't received a letter from my husband for almost two years. Dead, I thought, in a battle with casualties too massive for the bodies to be identified. I poured my grief into my poems. They were lovely, actually, odes to my beloved menfolk, spiced with a bit of vitriol against the war that had taken them. I told myself that sending the work to the newspaper was in further memory of my lost loved ones, not prideful preening. The *Vicksburg Gazette* published the poems. The Memphis paper picked them up, too, plus the *Crier* in Birmingham. They were well received. The editors clamored for more.

"So I wrote more. Each imagined the brave deaths suffered by our Confederate boys in the foreign North. How unfair it was to lose our sons, how cruel the North was to steal them. Over and over, I shook a raised fist at the war that had cheated love.

"But as time passed and my grief lost its white heat, and most particularly, when my child began to grow, my poems changed. I like to think what was once unhinged, rehinged. Each poem had a turning point where the lambasting of the enemy segued to a plea to move on. A suggestion that we pack up our sorrow and learn how to live with the world our war—and our defeat in that war—had created.

"The *Gazette* wouldn't print my new poems, nor would they share them with their regional colleagues. Oh, sure, they printed the first half of the poems, but not the second. Too long, they claimed. So I shortened the tirade to get more quickly to the plea that we quit whining and take our lumps as the strong people we were. The rejection was the same. When I finally shrank the ode section to three lines, the editor complained that they were hardly poems at all. I pointed out they were plenty of poems if he printed them in their entirety. The editor told me there would be no 'lump-taking.' He would never print the full poems, nor would any of his sister publications. The readers had absorbed my railing against the unfair war and would never concede that our cause was not noble. My writing had unwittingly created a myth of an angelic host of beautiful and brave soldiers who died for a war instigated by a cruel and unworthy enemy."

Bigmama looked into the distance, shrugged. "In a move to shut me up, the Magnolia Press Coalition invited me to their annual banquet, made me an honorary member, and gave me a medal for my work as the Poetess of the Confederacy."

I'll be damned. I remembered the story Elfy had told me in yet another attempt to besmirch her daughter-in-law. "That's why you slapped the president? Because they honored you for something you didn't intend?"

She smiled. "At least that much of my story survived." Then her eyes contracted with pain. "When I spewed my vitriol, I was immersed in grief. Surely that affords me some mercy. Grief and . . ."

She bit her lip, her forehead crinkling with consternation.

"Go ahead, get it over with," I advised. "Like a Band-Aid. Rippppp! That's what my Bigmama would say."

Instead of answering me, she untucked her journal and flipped the pages until she found her place. She adjusted an imaginary set of spectacles on her nose, and realizing they did not exist, brought the journal closer to her face. She read: "He should never have come back. We had our time together, our shard of happiness. We agreed to wrap it in cotton and never open it. He had never come and would not return. I did as he said. I smothered my sorrow and believed him gone forever. Even when I heard the front door open. Stilled at the creaking of the stairs. I did not consider the possibility of a key, an allowed visitor. I had been told by his own mouth that I must count on never seeing him again. So I did not. The door slowly swung open. I shot."

Closing the pages, she looked up at me, her face gray as granite. "I killed my husband, Etoile. The man I loved more than life itself, and I took that life while his baby slept in the cradle beside my bed."

My guilt melted like a sugar cube in the rain. Bigmama had killed someone she loved. Her very love. She had survived the war and birthed a child and holed up in her destroyed house only to shoot her returning husband. Hell's bells. I had killed a man I hated. Even in my line of ancestors, I was such a poser. Irrationally, I wanted to burst out laughing.

"Why did you do it, your novels?" I asked when I had calmed myself. "The family said you started writing when Jewel was a baby. What caused you to pick up your pen in the first place and create such a distorted truth? Why?"

We walked past a pot of lantana spilling onto the sidewalk. Its bitter scent swept along with us. A contented look settled on Bigmama's face, as if she were my own Bigmama and I had placed a fresh spiral notebook in her hand. "I wanted to write the truth. I would show those people to be the stupid, selfish, degenerate, lazy, uncouth, despicable, careless, combative, pig-headed, violent people they were. I put the most ignorant words imaginable in their mouths, the most uneducated thoughts in their heads. I tore into the paper and had to restart with a clean sheet over and over again. But every time, I kept my objective clear in my brain: show those who caused the war and sent my husband into harm's way to be absolute fools."

She wiggled her nose, perhaps a habit acquired during the weeks then months living in a dank cave. "But readers obstinately missed the point. They took the characters' words and thoughts as an endorsement. So I made my point again, only stronger. I would show them. Every time I missed the mark, every time my intent was perverted, they won again, sending me into a blind rage. Really, I lost my mind. The war, my fear, the shotgun pointed at the shadow of a shape. Other than my baby girl, I hated everyone alive."

During the telling, her posture had straightened. She was once again my Bigmama, formidable as iron. People flowed all around us. Not tourists, real people. The folks who lived on the West Bank or in the Broadmoor neighborhood or, every once in a while, in Gentilly. Residents. Not like me in my stretchy red jumpsuit ignorantly accusing my granny of ignorance. On a quest but turned all around.

I halted. We had arrived at the corner of Chartres. I looked behind us. You could see the spire of the cathedral rising over the roofline. Ahead of us was the famous Napoleon House. I reached out and touched Bigmama's arm. She emerged from her reverie and raised her gaze to mine as if she had forgotten I was there.

"If we're gonna screw up, we might as well burn that fucker down," I said.

Bigmama raised one eyebrow, which was the only lesson my mother ever taught me: Don't raise an eyebrow unless you're ready for a fight.

But a smile spread over her face until she out and out laughed—when had I ever heard my own Bigmama laugh?

She patted my hand, pressing my flesh to hers. "I do believe you are mine, child."

Maybe I hadn't screwed up this quest so bad.

The thing about counting chickens, those little suckers will turn around and sink their saw teeth into your flesh before you know what's happening.

Chapter 49

When the forces of the world banded together to defeat the great Napoleon Bonaparte, the emperor scratched his feather quill across vellum and abdicated. The victors—seated in Napoleonic chairs at a Napoleonic table and overseen by a gilt Napoleonic clock—exiled him to the island of Elba, where he would be sovereign emperor over a rock. He would fly the Napoleonic flag at what they called a principality of France and command a garrison of four hundred soldiers who he could order to stand on their heads while reciting the number of the enemy killed in each of his battles, if he wanted.

His son, however, could not be emperor in his stead. No, no, no, the winners said. Little Franz could not rule. His mother could not be regent. The King of Rome, as he was known, must abdicate too. (Sound familiar?)

As we know, Napoleon only stayed so long in exile. He escaped the island of Elba and entered France in triumph. King Louis XVIII fled (i.e., he ran away), and France was once again Napoleon's country. The world powers that had defeated

Napoleon were not happy. They were forced to defeat him again. Where? Waterloo, the famous ABBA site. JK. Napoleon abdicated. Again.

Now listen up. Here comes the important part.

When Napoleon and the powers that be were trying to decide what exile would look like in this do-over, Napoleon intended to make his new home in America.

Not simply America.

New Orleans.

In July 1815, Napoleon was set to take a ship to the Crescent City. He wanted a beignet. Or at least a city where, after his rough patch, he could land among a friendly crowd, as if his ass deserved a fluffy pillow.

Small problem. At the time Napoleon was evaluating his where-do-we-go-from-here options, the world was reeling in shock from America's victory at the Battle of New Orleans. The British did not want Napoleon exiling himself to New Orleans. Can you imagine that combination?

The British blocked Napoleon's ship from leaving port.

Back on the throne, poor ol' King Louis XVIII couldn't summon the courage to have Napoleon executed. So the British were forced to exile him again, this time to a much more remote island in the Atlantic called St. Helena. Napoleon wasn't happy. He would have preferred New Orleans by a long shot. He let word of his disappointment leak, and a plot was hatched to rescue him and sweep him off to New Orleans.

The plot wasn't pie in the sky. The richest man in New Orleans pinky swore to ensconce Napoleon at the grandest residence in the French Quarter. He would build a mansion and impress his idol from afar.

The plot fizzled.

The rich man abandoned the house, but a lesser-known merchant took up the cause and completed it with all the originally intended flair. It now housed the famous restaurant. But when I described Grande Red to the Napoleon House maître d', he shrugged. As we left, the bouncer at a dive bar next door stared at us.

"Big tall woman with a Minecraft head? Dude a bit older than him?" he asked, his arms folded against his chest.

When I nodded, he ushered us in. The place was built in the shape of a beehive. Bees were a symbol of the Napoleonic court because of their industry, or massive stingers, or due to their tummies looking exactly like Napoleon's. I don't know, maybe the knock-off bar was a pun on Napoleon's height. Anyway, the place was called the Little Bee.

Chapter 50

The last of the day's sun oozed down the wall of the Little Bee like warm honey. The peeling plaster cracked like an ironic smile: No telling how much money it cost to preserve the bar's decay.

The Quarter bar could not have been further from my Bywater neighborhood. I lived with community gardens and flamboyant graffiti and bicycles weaving through the streets, hipster cool. The bar, with its scarlet brocade and ancient maps and portraits of men with aquiline noses, was crumbling aristocracy. Hard to tell what of it was fake and what was real.

Clearing his throat, a waiter as old as the bubonic plague abandoned his vigil at one of the full-length French doors fronting the street. He wove around the Please Wait To Be Seated sign, and when he saw the dauphine, bowed, waving us to a café style two top table shoved against the wall. Tip-Top dragged over extra chairs. On either side of us, bar patrons spilled from the open French doors onto the sidewalk. A fat-bellied man balanced on the back legs of his spindly chair and saluted us with his Pimms cup.

We squinched around the tiny wooden table and ordered gumbo, shrimp remoulade, and, for me, an andouille sausage po'boy. The old waiter adjusted his black bowtie, his gaze never leaving the black and gold floor tiles as our order strung out. Not having eaten since breakfast at the apartment, we were starving.

At least I was. The others just wanted to sniff the aroma. Elfy, her dainty nose pointing toward the ceiling, was in hog heaven. Tip-Top seemed to be fascinated with a woman at the table next to us slurping oysters, shivering and sighing each time she swallowed. A drinker at the bar guffawed and shouted for his friend, "Pay up!" The waiter slid a cup of gumbo in front of me.

I scooped up the okra-filled gumbo, working my tongue to sieve pieces of crab shell. My heart sang when I chomped into the po'boy. The crunch of the crusty bread followed by the cloud puff inside. Smeared with Zatarain's Creole mustard and piled with Vidalia onions and sausage so spicy it made my lips tingle. Plus, a bag of Zapps, original flavor. The worst bar in New Orleans had better food than mediocre restaurants everywhere else in the world.

Beside me, the dauphine hummed the Marseillaise, sliding every once in a while into Dr. John's dilemma. Bigmama thrummed the table, studying the gold-filigreed bee that hung in a shadowbox on the wall above Louie's head. It was plastic. You could easily have missed it. The wall was papered with photos and framed memorabilia, some ancient, some as recent as 1960. The past flitted through the Little Bee with the same furtiveness as the small brown mouse currently weaving along the curb outside the French door, agile as a teenaged gymnast on the balance beam.

I paid it no mind—mice routinely ran through the ancient streets of the Quarter—but when the movement caught Louie's eye, he squinted. Quicker than I would have thought possible, he rose, strode through the door and kicked the little fella into the air like a football.

The mouse summersaulted, whiskers spinning, and splatted against the cobblestones where it lay, leg in the air, quivering.

Well, that was unsettling, his going out of his way to inflict cruelty. But then I saw my rat nemesis sailing away from my shovel. Why was one okay and not the other? A new thought floated into my brain. The dauphine, with his languid body and ruffled white shirt, had every intention of being in charge of this outing even before Tip-Top declared it his route to maturity.

The old waiter, as if receiving a signal, twitched his bushy mustache and shuffled over to our table. The soles of his shoes whispered like bedroom slippers on bathroom tile. He crooked his finger at the dauphine, inviting us to follow him.

Chapter 51

The Little Bee waiter led our group through an arched doorway into a hallway where a busboy clattered dirty silver into a rubber bin. From there, we passed through a pine door into a brick-lined room, easing shut the door behind us. I narrowly missed stumbling over a cot. A red velvet chair slouched beside the cot, an abandoned magazine in its seat. The space looked like someone's private quarters outfitted to look like what people here called a pied-à-terre and what I'd call a old-fashioned French love shack. When I pressed my palm against the shade of a standing lamp, it was still warm. I compared the indentation in the cot's blue ticking pillow to the size of the waiter's head but came to no conclusions.

The waiter motioned for the dauphine to take a seat in the velvet chair. As Louie moved the magazine and eased into the collapsed cushion, the waiter stood at attention as if before a throne. His white hair shone in the dusky room. He dropped his jaw like a rusted hinge and spoke loudly to rise above the noise of doves twittering in a wicker birdcage. He was reciting, but it was in French, so I had no idea what was so important.

"House of Bourbon," Elfy repeated, but I'd gotten that part. "House of Orleans, too. And that?" She cocked her ear to the brass-heavy music seeping from a cube-shaped speaker. "Beethoven's Eroica, dedicated to Napoleon."

If the look on Louie's face was any indication, the conversation wasn't going well. I tried to remember how our plan to return the dauphine to the castle was supposed to work. Tip-Top had said put him in charge of accomplishing a task, that was the key to maturity. But the dauphine was clearly in the driver's seat now, and he hadn't aged a day.

Maybe my life could provide a better road map. After all, St. Claude had said the dauphine was supposed to be me.

How had I grown up? Assuming I had, in fact, grown up from high school where mean girls drew pictures of my spiked hair on the bathroom mirrors and boys taunted me for wanting to learn what the teachers wanted to teach. I still had Tippy with me in high school, but I was taking care of her by then, not the other way around, which kept me pretty busy. A demented woman who loved knives and needles and pins was a handful. We made quite a pair—she would squirrel away weapons while I was at school, and in the evenings I would sniff out her hidey-holes. When she passed spring semester of my senior year, I clicked off her black oscillating fan and shut the door to her bedroom where as a little girl I had dreamed of the day when my hair, too, would be long enough to plait.

I had a weird reaction to Tippy's passing. Not grief for her, but a boomerang grief for my parents. That first year at community college, I sold off my life: auctioned Tippy's farm and closed up the Jackson mansion, hoping to unload it on someone. As the realtor nailed the sign in the yard, I imagined the grandchildren of my rat nemesis taking over the kitchen, chewing through the electrical wires until the house exploded in flames. Out of the blue, I felt myself wishing I'd had a normal childhood in my parents' home rather than a nomad's life farmed between grannies. Before that delusional nostalgia took hold, I gave the realtor the key to my parent's ranch house with the fiberglass carport and told her to sell that too. After that, I never again felt like a child. I was nineteen.

The dauphine, with his deeply thoughtful brow and puzzled chin-rubbing, was playacting. A boy patterning gestures he thought befitted a king or waving his arms in a way he hoped would be seductive. To grow up, did you have to lose the loves that had sustained you through your childhood, either voluntarily or have them wrenched away? Must tragedy strike the dauphine before he would quit pretending and actually become himself? And would our group have to be the ones to ram tragedy into his world? The smell of wet plaster clogged my throat. Leaky water ran down the wall, mixing with the air of intrigue and espionage and cabals, but this kid needed to get real.

"His mother wishes him dead." I broke into their conversation. "She cares more about her power and prestige than she does his life. We have to find her before she abandons him on this side of the timeline, and he dies."

Louie gave a dismissive wave in my direction. He tucked his black wavy tresses behind his ear. "She exaggerates. My mother is headstrong, but hardly ruthless. I—"

"If you have any information on where she might be, now is the time to share it." I glowered at the old man, my hand on the hilt of my sword. The waiter's cheeks sagged like wet dough. Overhead, the ceiling fan clicked.

Louie rose from the chair and draped an arm across my shoulder, where it lay heavy as a fire log.

I retracted my earlier observation. Louie was growing up. He had put on heft, his lithe body thickening. When we first met him, he had been taller than Elfy, which wasn't saying much. Now he was glancing down at me. His jaw could use a razor. Whatever we were going to do, we had to be quick. It did us no good to have a grown-up dauphine with no portal home.

"Mademoiselle, your eyes are too violet, your hair too raven for you to be so angry." He winked at me like a man who knew sex. "Could you grace us with a smile, perhaps?"

Okay, I also retracted my earlier claim that I liked this version of the dauphine.

As he smiled indulgently at me, I stepped back to free myself from the weight of his arm, but my brace caught on the leg of a side table. I slapped my palm on the table to balance myself, but the unsteady table sent a metal napkin canister clattering onto the tile floor.

At the sound, Bigmama drew her cudgel from her sash. Squinting, she aimed its heavy head at the old waiter's ear.

"No!" I called, waving my arms. These women were trigger-happy—or cudgel happy—attacking an old man waiter because I had stumbled.

Rearing back, Bigmama threw the cudgel underhand like a submarine spitting a torpedo.

The waiter was too nimble for her. He spun away from the cudgel as it smacked into a photograph of Dean Martin on the wall behind him. Its glass splintered into a thousand rays, and the cudgel bounced beneath the red velvet chair.

The waiter grinned, stretching his chubby lips like a cheap clown mask. The knife that had appeared in his hand glinted.

Chapter 52

I reached for my sword, but I was leaning over the table and couldn't get a grip. I hopped to shift my weight onto my good foot, but then I couldn't draw the blade off my hip. An alarmed Elfy shoved her hand into the deep pocket of her skirt, hunting for her pistol while Tip-Top, slow on the uptake, finally realized what was going on and unsheathed her knife. No one was quick enough.

"Vive le Bourbon!" the old waiter cackled and thrust his knife, the point descending toward the dauphine's heart.

The dauphine whipped off his cape and snapped it at the old guy. The tip of the cape zinged like a popping wet towel in a locker room. It caught the waiter in the eye, and his head jerked back. Staggering, he covered the eye with his palm and knocked against the wicker birdcage. The cage's pointy top dislodged and fell off. The doves inside flapped free, warbling in distress and shitting all over the place. One bird landed in the old guy's hair where it scratched with a vengeance, its legs working like pistons. The waiter slapped at his head, spinning in circles, his arms akimbo.

Looking back, I can see where they were trying to help. It wasn't their fault Elfy's pistol was already swinging to whack the old man on the temple. Or that her blow caused him to topple into Tip-Top's knife. And it sure wasn't their fault the claw of the fierce dove drove into the old guy's eyeball, piercing its jelly until it oozed. But when the old man's one good eye rolled back in his head and he fainted, falling to the floor and driving the knife deep into his now very still back, uttering his dying words, "Elissa." I almost swallowed my tongue.

"What the hell!" I shouted, brushing my hair off my face, and off my face again, and again.

Tip-Top ignored me, squatting to retrieve her knife, which she wiped on a clutch of napkins protruding from the broken dispenser. Elfy studied the downed man with her palm over her mouth as if she'd uttered a bad word. Only Bigmama stared at the body as if the outcome wasn't the best, and her look was more annoyance than upset.

"Guys!" This wasn't some make-believe minion that Bigmama had beat up. Or an ancient saint who popped in and out of the picture like bad internet reception. This was a man, a real live human being man person. Dead. "What the hell?"

"We saved the dauphine," Bigmama said, cool as the underside of a pillow. "Took all of us to do it. Including the dauphine himself. Mostly him. Not you, though."

"But he's dead!" I couldn't believe she was criticizing me for not participating in the old guy's murder.

"And none of us are," Elfy said, adjusting her skirt.

"You are, you're dead," I pointed wildly at her.

"You know what I mean, Etoile. We did exactly what was called for."

"You ruined it!" I seethed, opening and closing my fists. My face flushed hot. Had I ever yelled at my grannies in my entire life? But between them and the asshole dauphine, I was done. This couldn't be the way things were supposed to go. "Knock the knife from his hand. Tackle him. Pin his arms. Sit on him. Do not kill him."

"Didn't I see you attempting to draw your sword?" Tip-Top asked, pure puzzlement in her voice.

My chest constricted. Of course I had. I was as morally depraved as they were. All of us: heartless, blood-thirsty, devils.

I slumped onto the cot, and gripping the pillow, pressed it to my stomach. I was careful not to look at the poor waiter's body. "He knew Grande Red. He was our lead, our only lead. Does everything with y'all have to end in murder?"

"No, you ruined it."

The dauphine, who had been shifting from slippered foot to slippered foot, erupted at me. "I was winning his trust. I was assuring him we supported my mother, and we had to find her for her own protection. You," he said, disgusted. "You told him she was my enemy."

When I went to protest, Louie pressed his palms to his ears to drown out my reply.

In that instance, he was once again the young man we had first met, honestly grappling with how to be an adult in extraordinary circumstances. His distorted face shamed me. Teenagers. God, that terrible time when we had to experiment with who we would be and do it in front of everyone. I was supposed to be the adult in the room, the one in charge, and I had failed.

The decision I saw galloping toward me broke my heart. I had begun this adventure wanting nothing more than the together-again happiness of my grannies and me. An unstoppable group of awesome women. Whatever needed to be conquered, we would conquer it. Instead, we had beat up one nun and left another unconscious in a broom closet. Regressed the dauphine into an obnoxious, incompetent teenager. Killed an old waiter and shamed St. Claude about his sex life. We were a lethal force, all right. Lethal to all around us.

Violence was a place my grannies swam in like a cool green

lake. Beguiling dragonflies pranced on the lake's surface, leading you farther and farther from the shore, daring the silky water to rise above your chest, your chin, your nose. The violence could be hard to see, the way it called itself love. Stuffing a child full of your stories and your expectations that kept her from finding her own place in the world, that was violence. I loved my grannies, but they were about to drown me.

"I'm going to have to do this myself. Me and the dauphine. Alone."

Rising from the cot, I motioned for the dauphine to follow me out of the room.

Chapter 53

"What did you say?" Bigmama asked. Butt in the air, she had been digging her cudgel from beneath the chair, but she straightened, a look of astonishment on her face. "How on earth are you going to best Grande Red on your own?"

"Grande Red and her minion," Elfy chimed in. "Maybe all three minions, if they've regrouped. You'll be hopelessly outnumbered."

She stepped toward the dauphine, who had been following our back-and-forth. She straightened his cape, cocking her head to assess her work. Not satisfied, she slid her hands around his neck and stood up the collar. Resting her wrists daintily on his shoulder, she smiled full wattage at him. "Handsome boy, what do you want to do? Go it alone? Or stay with us?"

Blushing, Louie opened his mouth to respond, but this wasn't going to a vote.

"Y'all go back to the apartment and wait for me," I said, gently removing Elfy from the dauphine. "After we waylay Grande Red, we'll pass right by the apartment on our way back to the castle. We'll pick you up."

Pouting, Elfy set her small fists on her hips. Her eyes were smoldering, and for the first time, I saw where the family's lavender eyes, passed from generation to generation, had started. "That's a particularly poor idea, Etoile. St. Claude assigned us to help you. We may need to stay together for reasons you don't understand. It's too risky to split up."

"Maybe, but it's sure as hell too risky to stay together."

"Why are you doing this, Etoile?" Tip-Top sat on the saggy chair. "Sending us home to sit idly at the apartment? What do you know we don't?"

I couldn't believe she was questioning my motives. "This is my quest, my vision. I can't have underhanded motives because my hand is in charge of everything."

"So you abandon the plan we agreed to? You will no longer allow the dauphine to be in charge of his own destiny?"

It sounded sketchy when she put it that way, but I crossed my arms against her words. "I said what I said."

An astounded Tip-Top swung her head, scanning the room for someone to explain how I could be so dumb. Her plain brown face was so like my Tippy's. Not brown from birth but from choosing the fields, the growing cotton, and the sun as her companion. "Never bake a pie when the field is calling," my Tippy had quoted Tip-Top as she gently rolled a plum in her palms then peeled the juicy ball, thin skin clinging to her rusty knife. Her thumbs, creased with nicks from the past, performing this service for me because I didn't like skin on my plum. I was about to tell them I'd made a horrible mistake when Bigmama spoke.

"Very well." Bigmama returned her cudgel to her waistband. "Proceed on your own. You will have none of us nor our protection. Nor will you have a plan for getting this boy safely back to his time. But absolutely do it your way. Just don't come crying to us when you fail."

My second thoughts zipped away. So typical of Bigmama,

treating me like a wayward child. "Come on," I said to the dauphine. "We're wasting precious time."

"Wait a minute." Elfy pointed to the dead body, her finger curving with distaste. "We have to do something about that."

I had a moment of guilt—the old dude dying and with his last breath romantically calling for some long-lost love Elissa—but I rallied.

"Don't look at me," I said. "You made the mess. You clean it up."

Part VII

The Split

Chapter 54

The dauphine and I walked silently toward the docks. Overhead, the swooping birds blackened the evening sky while bells rang from a nearby Catholic Church, calling the faithful to Mass, calling down the night, calling me into a future where I saw no light.

Let's assume Louie and I cornered Grande Red, retrieved her false proclamation, and returned a grown-up dauphine safely to his time. One-hundred percent success, a job well-done. Our task finished, my grannies would evaporate with the dauphine, and where would that leave me? How could I return to constructing my pretender life?

All I had accomplished in the last two days was dig the hole of my life deeper. Instead of atoning for my inadvertent killing of my boss, I had become party to the killing of an old waiter. Probably a beloved icon of the city, been waiting tables at the Little Bee since Marie Laveau cast her first spell, everyone asked for him by name. Sure, he had come at the dauphine with a knife, and there was something screwy about him I couldn't put my finger on. But damn, life needed to quit giving me the choice of kill or be killed. And to top it off, I'd had a falling out with my grannies. I'd alienated the women who had been responsible for beginning the bloodlines that led to me being squalling and alive. How ungrateful was that. I was utterly alone again, but this time, I had inflicted the grief on myself.

I felt again how sorrow rent the fabric of time. When someone was snatched from you, and your grief swallowed you whole. Making you want so badly to return to the time when they were alive that your wailing threatened to pry apart the sleeves of time and slide back through, back to the good times, back into their love.

Grief shook me by the shoulders, rattling my teeth, and I longed for the moment when Tippy kissed my poor finger freed of its splinter. And Elfy declared my fever gone, and Bigmama slid her hand into mine and hitched us together until our rotation around the garden was finished. The longing was so fierce, the threat of time travel so real, I wondered, did grief call up this vision?

I was here again, in that place of the dangerous present. No point A to point B line to follow. Only me, in limbo between my chaotic past and blank future. Following the lead of a young man who had returned—again—to his first thought: His mother was seeking a ship to France.

The dauphine kicked his feet down the sidewalk, silent and surly. I was trying to remember how I had rebounded from my fits of teenage depression when the dauphine asked, his voice quiet, "Are you alive?"

"Ha! Yes," I said, triumphant. I definitely knew the answer to that.

Without looking in my direction, he asked, "Was the waiter Armand alive?"

"Yessss," I answered more slowly, since, thanks to us, the waiter was no longer alive.

"And he is now dead?"

"Certainly looked so."

The dauphine was quiet for a moment. The truth was, he'd learned a lot in a very short time. His father forced to abdicate. His mother putting him in danger by insisting he claim the throne. Just yesterday, he had been the protected, beloved son of the king, the next in line.

"I'm sorry, Louie, about all of this. I wish I knew how to make it easier for you."

He squinted at the sky. "He said my mother and her son had stayed at the bar until the wee hours of the morning, drinking, talking. Plotting. He wanted to know if I was her son too." He glanced at me sheepishly, embarrassed. "Younger brother, I told him. She misled Armand by claiming to be House of Bourbon."

"Isn't she House of Bourbon?" I thought the Wiki page had said the last dauphin was a Bourbon. "The Bourbon Revolution or restoration or refrigeration—something, right?"

Louie drew himself up. "I am House of Bourbon. She is merely my mother."

I remembered his declaration to his mother: "I will be king, and you will not." But as an adult, he had fully intended to abdicate the throne. Was I helping him defend his throne against his mother or helping him grow up so he could abdicate as he wished?

"Armand was a loyalist," he said, and I winced. I wished he would quit using the man's name. "He believed he was helping the House of Bourbon. He passed along valuable connections. To Elissa."

"His girlfriend?" That was odd.

"The *Elissa*. I imagine it's a ship at port."

"Seriously? She's really going to sail to France?"

He nodded, a lock of his bangs falling into his eyes, shifting him back to a boy on the cusp of being a man. No telling what turn we might take, but regardless of my grannies' theory of letting him make his own decisions, he still needed guidance.

Guidance, I'm saying, not a forty-ton family history dropped on his head like an anvil. A distinction my grannies never made.

As we took the steps to the Riverwalk, we were greeted with fog rolling in off the river like a low-budget Jack the Ripper film. The fog drifted, heaven's clouds come to earth. Now and again, without warning, pedestrians emerged from its embrace, droplets pressing their wet hair as if they were escaping a moment of passion.

Suddenly, out of the fog rose the tallest ship I had ever seen.

Chapter 55

Not just one ship, but three wooden sailing ships with towering masts and sails furled like bats hanging on the edge of the world.

"Holy shit," I exclaimed, nearing so I could see better. "I heard about this, but I hadn't seen it. You don't know this," I said to Louie, "because you've only been in the Marigny and the French Quarter, where everything looks the same as it did three billion years ago, but that." I pointed to the tall ships that resembled pirate vessels. "That is not normal."

"Did Armand call them to the city?"

"No, they're here for the three hundredth celebration of the founding of New Orleans. The tricentennial. It's been a year-long party. Lord, they're pretty."

The ships were crawling with sails. Sails in the middle, sails in the back, sails over the prow. I would have given anything to see the sails filled with air, puffing from the wind, but I guess they were asleep for the night. Even so, the masts were as impressive as sequoias stripped of their leaves in winter. Giant.

Majestic. Really, truly awesome.

It must have been a pretty regular sight for Louie, because all he asked was, "Which one is the *Elissa*?"

As we walked closer, I said, "I'm gonna guess the one flying the French flag."

Last in the row, the *Elissa* was smaller than the other two. More graceful, its masts not quite as massive. Faster, I bet.

"You think it's really sailing to France? And they will let your mom hitch a ride?"

We had arrived at the wharf's gangplank, through which you had to pass to get to any of the ships. I believe the ships had been offering spins around the harbor as part of the celebration. It had been on the news when they processed into town firing carronades, which were some type of gun cannon. The ships were Welsh or Scottish, and their crews were sailing fanatics. Seeing the ships in person, I kind of understood.

"If the waiter gave your mom the connection to the ship last night, that means she was planning on returning to France other than through the castle, which is strange. How did she already know the castle had disappeared?"

"Mother always has a backup plan," he said distractedly, eyeing the ships. "She looks not one but three steps ahead. For her, the future is a tributary of streams, and she readies herself to ford each one."

The wind ruffled Louie's hair. The fog had rolled on out, and the moon had emerged. It cast a glimmer on the river, a silver ladder beckoning the ships to climb.

"The first time I saw sails unfurled in the wind, I threw myself into the Seine," Louie said. "Father and I were in Paris, and the great ships were preparing to sail upriver. The crew climbed the rigging while the men on deck strained against the ropes, holding the canvas against the breeze. The men were strong, but the outcome wasn't assured. Could they keep the sails in check until the moment for release? Then suddenly, the sails filled. It was as if man's energy had been replaced by the breath of God. I wanted to be on the ship even if it meant jumping in the filthy river. After they fished me out, I began scheming to become a sailor. It wasn't going to happen, so I took to making ships in the bottle, but eventually I became disgusted with it. Cruel, it seemed, like trapping a hawk in an overturned bucket."

Behind him, the lighted spire of the cathedral rose bone white in the night. We were in a direct line from Jackson Square to the river. Surely I would have seen the masts of the ship from the window of the Cabildo this morning if they have been moored at the dock? Maybe they were out tooling around, impressing the locals. New Orleans was a city built for tall ships. We hadn't forgotten the splendor that made the French drop anchor at the bend in the river where the water plunged two hundred feet. We were a city of water made to be adorned by ships.

The ship creaked, and I imagined myself on its deck, my fist grasping the rough rigging. The captain barks orders. Waves slap the ship's sides, the spray mists my face. My lips part, tasting clean, essential freedom.

My spirits soared, and I bounced on the balls of my feet, clanking my sword against my brace. I wanted to sail from the city, waving goodbye as my ship headed into the horizon. What did I have to lose? No friends, no family, nothing keeping me here. The best use for the city right now might be a backdrop for escape. Plus, it wasn't running away if it was running toward, right?

Teetering on the moment of decision, I savored the exquisite build of tension before I burst out, "Let's go, Louie. Let's board her."

"Us?"

"Yes, us." After all, he needed someone to guide him. A chaperone. Who better to do that than me, who was him?

I tugged him up the gangplank, where a man emerged from a small hut.

"Tours are over," he said, waving his flashlight at our feet to check our progress. He swayed as if still on board a rolling ship. It was infectious, and I found myself swaying in the same rhythm. I sloshed to a halt.

"We want to board."

"No, ma'am. We're readying for morning departure. Maybe next time we come round, you can have a look-see." With a glance at my hip, he added, "Without your sword."

"We mean to book passage," I said, sounding like a Herman Melville novel.

"On the *Elissa*?" His weathered skin looked like it could walk off his face and stand on its own, causing a slight dip in my ardor. But all adventures carried costs.

"Yes, on your ship." I poked Louie with my elbow, encouraging him to jump in any time.

"We don't have passengers on the *Elissa*. Captain"—the man pointed at his chest with his wrinkled thumb—"and crew. That's it."

"Yet, we know an individual who intends to sail with you tomorrow." Louie's tone of voice implied that, while the captain wasn't quite a liar, he was definitely a withholder of the truth.

"Then your individual is crew, buddy." The captain clicked off his flashlight, turned on his heels, and slammed the door of his hut.

"We'll be back tomorrow!" I shouted after him. "Bright and early, you can count on it!"

"Where to now?" The dauphine wrapped his cape around him to ward off the chill entering the air. Behind him, the clouds in the sky glowed tangerine and gold, reflecting the neon of the French Quarter.

"Where else do you go to kill a night in New Orleans? Bourbon Street."

"Bourbon Street?" He pivoted to follow me, cape swirling. "Ah, of course the royal family would have a street in the city."

"Only the most famous street in town." Though I never did

the street. Couldn't, not if I wanted to succeed at being a true New Orleanian and not a mere pretender.

"And that is where we are going?"

"Moths to a flame, dear boy. Moths to a flame."

Chapter 56

The stage lights of Squiggles Bar turned the dauphine's face cotton candy pink. He was eating french fries for supper. With lots of "sauce." Ketchup, you and I might call it.

The metal cover band was taking a break so we could actually hear each other talk. The damp beer smell embedded in the wooden tables and wooden chairs and wooden floor was almost overwhelming. Plus, cigarette smoke. And weed. We'd had no trouble getting Louie in. If I'd had to guess his age, I would put it at nineteen, twenty. Old enough that the bouncer merely grunted as we passed, unwilling to take on the tall young man who so recently had been a newly hatched teenager. I didn't know if Tip-Top's decision-making theory was working or if time was passing at warp speed for him in this reality.

He swerved his french fry through the sauce and squirted more on his plate. He had a dollop of red in the corner of his mouth, saw me looking, and licked it clean. I nervously pinged the tines of my fork against the table.

Louie had just told me I reminded him of his mother.

"You don't listen," he said. "You pretend to, but you don't. You allow others a say, but that's only to get on with whatever you want. The others are talking, and you can't wait to jump in. Mother hides it better. You're too impatient."

"You think?" My blood was warming. "Your mother is willing to put the risk of her brilliant plan—let's make New Orleans a free-standing protectorate of France—on you, her son, who will die if she's wrong. I'm trying to enable you to live the life you want. I'm thinking of you. She thinks only of herself."

He wiped his fingers on his napkin. "You're talking motive. I'm talking approach. You might have better motives, but you shove others aside to reach your goals, exactly as she does."

I blanked for a moment as St. Claude's words whooshed into my brain. At the beginning of all this, the saint had said all actors in my vision were me, or versions of me. Was Louie right? Was Grande Red in all her regal awfulness, me?

Louie took the opportunity of my silence to lean his weight on the table and raise his right index finger. "Do not mistake me. No one rivals my mother in cruelty. For example."

He paused, tapping his finger against his mouth, a device, it seemed, to make sure he had my attention. I was so transfixed by his easy assumption of authority, the sophistication growing in front of me, I had to force myself to pay attention to what he was saying.

"We had a groom once who loved mother's bay stallion more than life itself. The groom would pamper that horse, brushing it until its hide shone. The Divine Emperor, that was the horse, but Max called him the Imp. The Imp got carrots at night, a fresh bed of hay. He was beautiful, the color of burned caramel, with plaited licorice for a mane. And smart. I didn't know horses could be so smart until I saw Max put the Imp through his paces. Mother told Max the horse would be his as soon as Father found a proper stallion to replace it. Then she told Father if he ever bought her anything other than a mare, she would slit the Imp's throat. Max labored for years in the vain hope that he would one day own that stallion. That is cruelty defined."

"What was she hoping to gain?" I couldn't see where being an asshole to the groom benefited his mother one way or the other.

"Loyalty. The man had never threatened to leave, never voiced any unhappiness with his position. But Mother saw an opportunity to tie him to her completely, and she took it. She revels in what is to her a game. To have used hope, this delicate, bobbing thing that keeps us alive, to achieve her dominance—well, that made her trickery that much sweeter."

I picked at the sleeve of my jumpsuit, remembering the moment I realized my boss had one-hundred percent tricked me. I was still struggling on the grass beneath the rattling pecan leaves when the truth crystalized before me. The extra time he spent editing my copy. Going out of his way to credit my ideas in group memos. The raise he championed, even though I hadn't been a year at the job. The attack became inevitable, a dull, *How did I not see this coming*? My gnome psychiatrist wouldn't give my guilt two minutes of airtime: Never blame yourself for being deceived by a con man. They know they're running a con. You don't.

"I hate sneaky sneaks." I downed my Brandy Alexander, licking the inside of the glass to get the last drop. All around me, the noise of the bar returned: the band tuning up, the toilet flushing as a young man emerged from the can, a group of drunk bridesmaids (God bless them) singing about Lizzo's DNA. I'd be damned if I'd knowingly be Grande Red in any form or fashion. "So tell me what you've been saying that I haven't been listening to?"

"There's no point in our returning to the *Elissa* tomorrow. Mother isn't getting on that ship."

I banged my empty glass on the table. "Since the moment you arrived in this form"—I waved at his body—"you've been convinced your mother intended to sail back to France. 'She's going to the docks.' 'I need to get to the docks.' 'Mother has made passage on the *Elissa*.' Now you're saying she isn't sailing to France after all?"

"Yes, I thought that, but you heard the captain. It's only him and the crew. Mother isn't going to crew a ship."

"So . . . what?"

"So who put us onto the ship?"

I was about to argue that no one had gotten us on the ship—that was the problem. We hadn't actually boarded it, then I understood. "Who told us she intended to board the ship? The waiter, you mean?"

He gave me a *catch-up here* look.

"Are you saying your mother told the waiter to tell us that? The waiter was a plant? A red herring?"

"No, I'm not convinced he was a willing accomplice. Perhaps he believed those were Mother's plans. But yes, she wanted us to continue to believe she was desperately searching for a way to return to France. Distracting us so we wouldn't look to the side." He held his palm to the side of his face where he waffled it in the air.

"And if we did look to the side, what would we see?"

"My mother, following us."

Chapter 57

The thought of Grande Red tricking us—again—lit gunpowder inside of me. I cursed myself for ever saying I wanted to be her, admired her, yearned to occupy space in the world the way she did. Sticking up for yourself didn't need Grande Red's cruelty, and I'd burn in hell before I patterned myself after her. In that crackling flame, any pretense I had at being other than exactly what I was burned away.

I had spent the last three years acting like New Orleans was a lover whose eye I had somehow managed to catch even though he was way better-looking than me, way more popular, and could actually tell a joke without tripping on the punchline. I twisted myself in knots to impress this arbiter of cool, secretly monitoring its reactions, taking my signals from it so that I was always a beat behind in my laugh or sneer or slow-eyed blink.

Despite my unwavering devotion, all I had managed was a litany of Mardi Gras don'ts: Don't eat king cake out of season. Don't stand beside a cute kid if you want to snag any loot. Don't embarrass yourself by shouting, "Throw me something, mister."

I called street medians the neutral ground, downtown the CBD, and wouldn't say *N'awlins* upon pain of death, which I almost caused to two joggers rather than straddle my car on the streetcar line like a cow on the train tracks in a Grade-B Western. But I rejoiced when I stalled like a local in the buzz of traffic on the Crescent City Connection until the sun collecting in my car and the swiftly flowing river lulled me into a daze, as lost in reverie as the fly twapping against the rearview window of my car. I was a true New Orleanian, me. And lest we forget, I sold that perfectly good car so I would have no choice but to rely on my bike, because hey, the Bywater.

Ever since I dragged my bruised, bleeding self across the Spillway into this city so old it could treat its racist KKK period as a blip on the radar screen, I had spent my waking hours confused about which way was up. Literally, there was no north and south, east, and west in this locked-down, secret-handshake of a city that wrapped around the bend in the river like a witchy phase of the moon. "Upriver," they said, and I had to think: Which way does the river flow? I was embarrassing myself. Prostituting and prostrating myself. Running after a mirage I would never catch. It needed to stop.

Because, you know what? Threading yourself to this city was playing a fool's game. I was spinning on a roulette wheel. Every time I thought I was stepping on red fourteen, the wheel spun, and my foot landed on black twelve. I would always be a Mississippi rube who ran away to the city just like every unhappy Mississippian had done since God was a toddler. I could live forever with the morning-afternoon-evening swooping birds and traveling fog and fast-flowing river and spinning hurricanes of New Orleans, but I would never understand it or its people. And the more I acted like I did, the bigger pretender I became.

As long as I was confessing, you wanna know the pitiful why of it? Why I had been contorting myself into a smaller and smaller box like a chained Houdini about to splash into the depths? It wasn't just my desire to step out of who I was and become someone else. We all wanted that, right? Well, not me, not all the time. Sometimes I was perfectly okay with who I was. It was the why of me chasing after New Orleans that really sucked. My grannies—that forever line of awesome women who birthed and raised and continued the family in me—had loved on me as purely and faithfully as anyone could ask. About as flawed, too, but what did that matter? Their wisdom was priceless. They just couldn't separate their brilliance from the knee-jerk reaction violence taught them.

I can now see in every iteration how Bigmama retreated into her imaginary world, Tip-Top forever prepared for the attack, and Elfy slid into guile at the slightest provocation. I got it. You ask me to get over my attack, and I can feel myself hugging it to my breast as if it were a beloved rag doll—*it's mine and you can't have it*. I had to give that up, or violence might as well be sewn into my DNA because I would pass it along and along forever.

That's not what sent me fleeing to New Orleans. My grannies did the best they could. They tried with their whole hearts to prepare me for the world, and then they died. They fucking died. They left me alone. That's who I was: a little girl crying over her dead grannies. Running away to a new world of sugary sweet pralines where I could ignore the salty tears of its oysters and pretend to be someone who could survive on her own.

Somehow the Bywater discovered my weakness and fulfilled my deepest desire—to again be loved. It concocted an entire quest to justify bringing my murderous ancestors back to me simply because it felt sorry for me. I'm saying, the Bywater felt sorry for my pitiful ass. And everyone knows hate isn't the opposite of love. Pity is.

I had been going about this all wrong.

I could no more jettison my grannies in a fit of pique at their killing a floppy-cheeked waiter than I could say with a straight face that I wasn't from Mississippi. Not if I wanted to survive this quest and become who I was meant to be. The real me. I could not quit being a pretender by pretending I didn't need my grannies.

As I admitted this, the dauphine transformed before my eyes.

The teenage boy who had skittered away from his mother's wrath and chose Elfy shifted. The contours of his face—the high cheekbones, the man's heavy skull, the narrowing jaw devoid of lingering baby fat—clicked into place like the tumblers of a lock sliding into its one true combination. That which was meant to be all along found its home, and the adult dauphine was back.

Part VIII

Re-Past

Chapter 58

"Hullo," I said, trying not to stare at the dauphine. Behind him, a Jell-O-shot chick wearing her African scarf as a skirt did the staring for me. The dauphine was more handsome as an adult than I remembered, his face more contoured, his eyes a deeper violet, his shoulders broader beneath his cape. Or maybe I was just glad to see him. "You have returned."

He looked the way I felt under the pecan tree when my boss released the pressure on my neck, and I woke from the blackout. Everyone knows about waking up and not knowing where you are, say, after a concussion. But when the tree limbs came into focus over my head, I didn't know who I was. Not a clue. I couldn't remember if I was in school, or married, or if I was working in an office in a big glass high rise. I couldn't remember any decisions I had made in my life, and lying there, I felt the walls holding up my life slowly lean and fall. Instead of being upset, I was relieved to walk away free.

Until I began to hurt.

"Do you hurt?" I asked the dauphine.

The focus in his eyes switched to me. His gaze roamed over my face, lighting on my chin, my mouth, my nose, my forehead, and drifting back down to my eyes. He stretched an arm to the side, flapping it up and down like a bird. "My arms were fat as capons trussed for roasting." He balled a fist, tightening the muscles in his forearms, then released it, splaying his fingers. "My fingers were fat little worms."

His neck was thicker than Louie's, his ears less delicate, that unique arrangement of parts that made a man out of a boy. On the table, the salt shaker gleamed in the bar's pink light, and the dauphine seized it, rocking it back and forth, throwing crystal light into the air.

"When I was a child, eight or nine years old, my father took me to the Royal Mint," he said, staring at his own personal light show. "The officer led us through to the stamping room, where we met an inspector. Wanting to prove the power of the presses, the inspector showed me his fingers, which had been smashed into a mass of flesh by the press. 'Powerful,' the inspector said, 'but fallible.' He pulled a double-stamped coin from his pocket. The king's face was there but shadowed by a second outline of his face. Two faces, like an echo distorting them both. At Napoleon's death mask, when I as a toddler ran toward me, for a moment I was that coin."

He abandoned the salt shaker and wiped his palm on his pants. Slinging his arm across the chairback, he stared at me. The look on his face was hard to read. Not quite hostility. Challenge, maybe? As if I had created an unwinnable situation for him.

Guilt made me flush. Had he, in his altered state, perhaps seen the truth of why he was here? Maybe I should confess I was the author of this fever dream, and he was me or I was him or whatever. Then I saw Claude failing to tell me Grande Red was the dauphine's mother and his coconspirator. Not to mention the still-murky scene when the castle had to step up to keep her from leaving without the dauphine. I could not trust anything the saint had told me. All I could safely tell the dauphine was what I knew firsthand, which was precious little.

"I'm sorry you've gone through all of this." I knew that much.

The dauphine rubbed his fingertips together, as if trying to suss an answer out of the air. He'd done that as a baby, rubbing the pads of his fingers. Other things stayed with him too, like his furrowed brows, so cute in a baby. Now that I had met his earlier selves, I could see the continuity in who he was all the way back to when I held him as a silky soft child in my arms.

The dauphine cut off my thoughts. "No matter. As you say, I'm back. Where do we stand with my mother?"

Where indeed?

"We thought she was trying to find a way back to France because the castle wouldn't let her leave without you. But you said she only wanted us to think that. In reality"—I winced at the word—"she's following us."

"Aha." He rearranged his butt in the chair. The chairs were small and wobbly, with spindles that poked your spine. A dude in a tank top on his way to the bar paused to fluff the fringe on the dauphine's cape. The dauphine retrieved his property as the metal band screeched into a song, blasting a hole in my eardrums.

Standing, he tugged me out the side door to a fenced alley with too full garbage cans spilling trash and a dead banana plant wilting against the fence. My ears rang with leftover music, and I worked my jaw, which didn't help. I turned up a blue bucket and sat, suddenly aware midnight was a long time ago.

The dauphine leaned against the wall, crossing his legs at the ankle. "Mother doesn't carry her own weight, so the . . . your . . . my conclusion makes sense."

"What do you mean, carry her weight?"

"Mother always makes someone else do the work. She wants me to sit on the throne so she can retain power, but it is I who carry the risk. It is I who must do the hard work of ruling. Mother is quite adept at riding coattails. If you're saying we once thought she was working to return to France and now believe she is following us, she undoubtedly believes we will figure out how to return. When we do, she'll knock us out of the way and take it."

He caressed his forearm, and I wondered if he loved himself more since he'd lost himself. We are all seriatim versions of ourselves, but most of us aren't aware of it.

"Or to put it another way," he continued, "she is a hyena that eats the meat others kill. I expect she is lurking in the shadows until an opportune moment when she can pounce and take advantage of our accomplishments. What have we accomplished?"

Chapter 59

Having no immediate answer to the dauphine's question, I loosened my sword, which was poking into my hip, and laid it on the alley's uneven bricks. Kicking out my leg, I groaned at the pleasure of the weight releasing from my brace. Out on the sidewalk, Bourbon Street was turning sloppy. It was well past the time when casual revelers had departed. Lone drunks weaved, occasionally thunking from the curb into the street, as they tried to look brave and unafraid. Not too long ago (as in five minutes), I would have judged them. But I no longer cared about impressing the city. In the morning, the street would be re-ordered. The vomit hosed off, used condoms swept up, overturned pots righted with only a few bruised hibiscus.

"We have accomplished nothing." I answered the dauphine's question. "We have been chasing after your mother, following the distractions she laid down for us. We ran back to the castle to head her off at the pass, but the castle was gone. St. Claude said it's on our side and disappeared to keep your mom from using it to return. You were convinced she was going to the docks to set sail, but we ran into a brick wall there, and you changed your mind. That led to your theory she was following us, and we came here. Oh, and we killed an old waiter."

"I understand my confusion. I cannot imagine a younger me being able to look clear-eyed at Mother." The dauphine paced up and down the alley, ignoring the death in our wake. "Her idea of a new monarchy is politically brilliant, a win-win for our family and the Duke of Chartres. We would own our own country, and I would be removed from royal controversy for good. None of that shuffling between friendly monarchies until some rogue cabal decided to pin its hopes on me, and the friendly country turns hostile. If I'm here in the New World, there'd be no periodic outbreaks of Bourbon fever or barons rustling up an army with cries of 'Vive la Bourbon!' whenever the Duke of Chartres levied a new tax on snuff boxes or some such. I assure you, the duke would be asking where he needed to sign."

"But?"

"But Mother's tears in the tower were tears of frustration. The king, her husband, had lost his power. She was desperate to transfer that power to me. But if I lost it, would she admit defeat? Or would she search around for the next powerful man to attach to? And if she were successful, if she found her next patsy, what would she do if that man's power depended on me being out of the picture? Where would her loyalties lie then?"

I imagined what he was describing. The two of them, mother and son, back in the tower. His mother, desperate, realizing her powerful men were dropping from the royal branch like dead leaves. It finally sinks in that her future is in free fall . . . until she spies her chance at a new alliance, one that didn't include her son. What would she do?

The dauphine pressed his back against the brick wall, his palms flat on the rough surface as if he lined up in front of a firing squad, and my heart broke for him. I'd had a terrible mother, but she hadn't been willing to kill me. Other than by neglect, I mean, which was a major big difference.

"Oddly mothered," the saint had said, and I'd thought, yeah, buddy, that's an understatement. But the dauphine was convinced his mother was open to killing him for no reason other than her own power. How was the son of such a mother even sane?

Or was he?

Was I?

"I don't know how a mother could ever act like that."

"I will tell you this one story about my mother." He slid down the brick wall to squat on his haunches. His embroidered shoes wrinkled, and I wondered: Where did the clothes go when he transformed? Where did they come from when he returned? Where did they wait while he was gone?

As if he felt my mind wandering, he slapped the ground. For the first time in all his incarnations, I saw true anger flashing from him. "One story to explain her to you. I will tell you why I say she wishes me dead. Then I will never speak of her in intimate terms again."

Chapter 60

"I was a young boy, six years old and still in short pants. Every night, my valet put me to bed in a pleated white gown. One Sunday, we processed into church for the christening of my young cousin. Ever after, I believed I slept in a baptismal gown, my soul made new each morning. But a demon began invading my dreams. To this day, I believe too much religious fervor conjures demons as often as it does saints."

Moonlight bathed his taut face. A breeze murmured in the ragged banana plant, rustling its leaves. "The line between the two can be very thin."

"Thin as a communion wafer," I offered.

"A plucked brow," he said, but the smile slid from his face.

"The demon haunted me every night. Long after the rest of the castle slumbered, I woke drenched in sweat. A nameless, formless terror bolted me awake. I could feel it hanging in the room, heavy as soot. The demon—or the terror—sucked my breath. Panting like a dog, I fell to my hands and knees and crawled into the adjoining room where my *nounou* lay like a vampire in her coffin. Nothing roused Nanny from her sleep. I would curl on the rug beside her bed, and she, wakening at dawn, would scoop me up and pour me back into my bed.

"One night, I'd had enough, and I gave up on Nanny. When the terror struck, I crept along the corridor to Mother's room, where I slid through the door. I would never dare approach her bed. I could not even allow her to sense I was there. But I knew deep within my bones no demon would invade her sanctuary, not if it wanted its head to stay attached to its neck. I secreted myself behind the tapestry of the killing of the dragon."

His gaze swept my red jumpsuit just long enough for me to understand that, yes, the stained glass of my Bywater castle was the tapestry of his childhood home.

"Mother wasn't alone. Odd noises emanated from her bed. Gasping and low snickering. I had never heard my mother snicker and wouldn't have thought such a thing possible. The other did not sound like my father. I pushed the rough tapestry aside and peeked out."

The whole time the dauphine told this story, he held his fist to his breastbone, rubbing it with his knuckles as if trying to comfort the young boy within.

"I knew the man, though I hadn't a clue what he was doing lying sprawled on top of mother as if he'd tripped. He was the king's archer, a man with an arm so sure Father insisted he march before him in every public appearance. Alexandre would swing his bow from side to side, daring anyone to attack. He wore his long blond hair in a braid, and I, the black-haired son of a black-haired man, thought he was an angel dropped by God's fingers to protect my papa. As he tried to get up from the bed—up and down, up and down—the mattress squeaked like a mouse."

I saw in my mind's eye the hapless mouse somersaulting onto the French Quarter cobblestones. All of God's children paid for our childhood hurts.

"Several days later, I was riding with Papa, seated on the

saddle in front of him, holding the reins, pretending to guide the horse. We were in the open fields, the weeds whipping the horse's legs, the sun beating our bare heads. As we cantered, my bottom thumped in the saddle. In my enthusiasm, I shouted, 'Pierce me with your arrow, harder, harder.' Papa corrected me. "No, son: 'Pierce him with your arrow, truer, truer.' For this was the chant that the arrow guardsmen sang when assembled for parade.

"I told Papa this was not the way Mother said it when she was using the archer for a blanket. That was the explanation I had arrived at. Mother's blanket had slid off the bed, and the marksman was protecting her from the nighttime cold because that was his job, to protect my family.

"We slowed to a jounce, the saddle creaking, then Father, 'Whoa'd' the stallion to a halt. He asked me to repeat what I'd said. I grew shy, afraid my blanket explanation was stupid. But I repeated it.

"A retinue trailed us, and I've often wondered if Papa feared they heard us. Otherwise, without a witness, he could be free to ignore my story, pretend no betrayal had occurred, no treason."

The door from the bar opened, and noise spilled out. A server glanced at a lopsided chair beside the door with a pile of cigarette butts at its foot, but one look at the dauphine squatting against the wall, and she popped her head back inside.

"My father was a good man." The dauphine tugged a tuft of weeds from between the bricks. "When we rode, he would fit my boot into the silver stirrups and say, 'Up you go, *mon fils*.' He never let his stallion thunder into a grouse's nest, afraid for the young ones. But he could not tolerate the chafing of uncertainty. After our talk, I saw him circling the garden, circling as the sun cast its shadow around the sundial.

"The next time I saw the blond-haired archer, he was tied to a post. His fellow marksmen were arcing flaming arrows into the night. Each time they let loose a volley, they stepped forward five paces and shouted, 'Pierce me with your arrow, harder, harder.' From my nursery window, I watched until the flaming arrows found their mark. Their sharp tips pierced Alexandre. The flaming shafts charred his porcelain skin, and to preclude any chance of survival, the wax smeared on his body held the flames tight. Mother sat at Papa's side on a makeshift stage. Even from my distance, I could see the rage engulfing her.

"How she knew it was me, I don't know. Maybe Papa gave me away as he laid his claim of infidelity. She never mentioned my inadvertent betrayal. Yet, whenever I failed to do as I was told, she would hiss, 'You must try harder, harder.'"

The dauphine's cheeks had spotted with color, as if a woman had smudged them with a lipstick kiss. My brace felt heavy on my leg. I had wondered who the dauphine had killed. Now I knew. Like each of us, the violence in his life was not of his making. But all the same, he carried the burden of another's death.

The dauphine stood. "Over the years, I've seen glimmers of the depth of Mother's obsession, but this trip . . . It has shown me the rot at the center of our relationship. Mother will never admit it, but she will not be satisfied until she avenges her lover. She creates excuses and weaves elaborate schemes and tangles herself in knots to hide her intent, but the truth is, she won't quit until she has killed me in return."

Chapter 61

Staring at the dauphine's rigid body, I remembered feeling like Narcissus. Now I understood my love wasn't of my own face. I was obsessed with grieving, my sorrow. I saw it reflected in him, but something was missing. If the dauphine was my twin brother from another mother, who in his life had loved him? Who were his three grannies? Who were his saviors?

Dear God, surely it wasn't me?

"I am so sorry." I went to stand beside him but did not touch him. "There's nothing I can say to make it better. Just know we're gonna do whatever we can to help you."

He turned toward me. His eyes were shadowed, as if he had begun to withdraw into a decision made. "She lays a choice at my feet. I go along with her scheme or forever be the pretender to the throne."

"The what?"

"The pretender. With another seated on the throne, as long as I am alive, I am the legitimate pretender. I am he who claims legitimate title. The Duke of Chartres will call himself Louis

Philippe I, king of France, yet the legitimists will recognize me as the proper line, which is why the king will forever wish me dead, the risk my mother refuses to acknowledge. I will be viewed as the true descendant of Charlemagne, he who should be seated on the Capetian throne. *Je suis le pretendre.*"

"Are you serious?"

He twitched his nose in annoyance.

"Don't you get it?" I balled my fists in excitement, digging my fingernails into my palm. "I am the pretender."

"To what throne, pray tell?" he asked in deep disbelief.

"To the throne of cool? Fitting in? Belonging?" I threw my hands in the air. "Surely this means something." I limped in a circle in the narrow alley until I realized I was imitating the dauphine's pacing, and I halted, facing him.

"Listen to me. I am figuring this out as I go. Not just life, but this." I waved my hands up and down his body. "Why you're here. What it all means. But St. Claude, lying trickster that he is, told me way back at the beginning that I might want you dead."

He startled, quickly glancing at my prone sword.

"No, no." I waved my palms in denial. "I don't want any harm to come to you, I promise. But why would he even say that? I thought, well, I'm not a fan of boorish male behavior, so maybe you were destined to do something that would set me off. Or maybe I had a deep-seated hatred of my masculine side. But what if he was trying to say it's me I want dead? The real me. Kill it, enter the pretender."

I rubbed my forehead. "No, that's not it. I already know all that. Something about what comes after sorrow. Clear-eyedness, as you said. Admitting my grannies were less than perfect."

He barked out a laugh.

"Don't be rude. My grannies worked hard to make up for my lack of parents. My mom and dad, they hated me wanting their love when they only wanted to love themselves. With them AWOL, I had no one reflecting me back at me, you see?"

He gazed at me like I had sloshed into psychobabble, and maybe I had, but I forged ahead.

"I was me, alone, with no context of who I was. My grannies tried to fill that void, but the past has to be a jumping-off point, not the landing place. Since you've arrived, I've come to see I need to accept them, love them despite their terrible failures. And what if you're the same?"

He was obviously trying to work out what I was saying, but he didn't have the facts to succeed. I wasn't about to fill him in. (I conjured you, and you might be me, but even though I've seen you as a baby and a teenager, I think you're hot.)

"I realize the danger of wading into someone else's life," I said. "But the circumstances are a bit special here. What I'm saying is, what if you need to see the same truth as me? What if your mom, no matter how misguided, is trying to give you the context of yourself? She made the same mistake my grannies did, turning the past into a straitjacket. I mean, I listen to your story, and I hear the person she hates is your dad, not you."

I held up a palm to forestall his interrupting. "She's eager for him to abdicate, not you. Humiliate him, not you. Maybe she was sincere when she said she was afraid you couldn't survive as a non-royal. The adults, they all screw up, but they don't hate us."

His considering look disappeared. "You may be able to delude yourself, but I will not entertain such a fairy tale. I have told you the depth of her hatred of me. I can never have a relationship with my mother. Your truth is not mine."

"Okay."

I could tell he was surprised by my quick capitulation, but I had to take care of my own little red wagon. "Come on." I tugged him by the sleeve.

"Where to?" he asked.

"I need to reunite with my grannies. Now, before it's too late."

As we left for my apartment, we passed a female clown

juggling plastic seals in front of a swaying, drunken crowd. The group would probably return to Omaha or Cleveland and tell folks how weird New Orleans was, when they were the ones on the sidewalk watching a ratty clown clumsily drop toy seals at five o'clock in the morning.

The rounded cobblestones humped against my instep. Above us, the early morning moonlight scoured the sky of dust, bringing clarity.

"Too bad the idea of New Orleans becoming a French protectorate won't work. It's a tad settler colonialism, but we're already settled, right? I bet France would give us a lot less toxic history."

The dauphine glanced at me, surprised. "You would give up your heritage?"

I waited until a delivery truck—rolling down the narrow street like an attacking tank, clattering and rumbling—passed. "If New Orleans hadn't been part of America, maybe it wouldn't have fought in the Civil War. No Reconstruction or Lost Cause Myth leading to a hundred years of violence." I thought of all the jazz artists fleeing to Paris to escape the racist hate. "No segregation. Maybe not even any slavery that led to all of that."

"And 'segregation' is?"

"Race laws designed to keep African Americans inferior in rights to White folks."

"That is not the New Orleans I know." He ran his fingers down a stretch of iron fence. Ahead of us, a statue stood stark against the gray sky. "New Orleans lets race move fluidly. Free People of Color. Creoles. The native born, as well as we Europeans. Similar to my home."

"Exactly, but it didn't stay that way. Maybe America was bad for New Orleans."

"Surely you are not again suggesting I trust my mother?"

"No, of course not."

Ahead of us, a line of folks on the sidewalk swiveled their heads, bird-dogging the scent of scorched coffee that always wormed itself through the air along N. Peter's Street. Why did we want to locate the source of a smell? What did its origins matter? But every morning, the same burned coffee from the roaster swiveled the same heads.

"Dauphine, listen to me."

The dauphine cocked his head. "Do I recall advising you to address me as Louis?"

"Actually, Louie."

"I prefer Louis."

"Louis. You love New Orleans. You said it first thing when I met you. I know it's hard to admit someone you're mad at might have a good idea. But honestly, what's wrong with Grande Red—your mom, I mean—her idea about tucking New Orleans under France's wing? It's exactly what you said you wanted. You relocate over here, it puts you out of the new king's hair. Your mom's happy. You're happy in the city you love. The city gets a new shot at the future."

The dauphine was quiet.

"What?" I asked after a moment.

"I told you why I could not agree to my mother's plan. I have made clear it threatens my life. Yet, you cannot help yourself. You are obsessed with pitching forward and now you advise me to do the same, to abandon what I know is right."

His violet eyes were clouded. Not with anger, with pity.

"I must grant you grace. After all, you did not have St. Claude to lecture you on the selfishness of such a stance. To drill into your head your duty to take up the responsibility of your life. I'm sorry for that, but it is too late for me to teach you."

He began to walk away.

"Hey!" I trotted after him. "Where are you going? We have to take care of my grannies."

"As you say, your grannies."

"But I promised the saint—"

He whirled around, flushed with anger. He pointed his elegant finger at me and said, "Do not follow me."

"I can't leave you." Sure, he was walking away from me, not I him, but it still felt like abandonment.

At the intersection of Chartres and Port, the dauphine strode the wrong way down a one-way street then quickly turned—another wrong way—up Royal. Perhaps two wrong ways made a right way. Thunder rumbled in the distance. It was October. It never rained in October. I approached the intersection and kept going. Three blocks later, I was at the foot of Montegut staring at where the castle had been. Now, not even the post-Katrina house sat on the empty lot.

No one was in sight. The dauphine hadn't run away, but he'd certainly walked away.

I was alone.

Chapter 62

I sat on the curb, chin in palm, deliberately not looking at the empty, castle-less lot. The sun boiled up like soup on the stove, annoyingly happy to be day again.

I had been stabbed with harsh words and then abandoned by a man I was trying my best to save.

Guess my best wasn't good enough. Too busy pitching forward, according to the so-called dauphine.

A dying bird flapped its wings in the gutter. When I was little, Tippy gave me a bumpy leather pouch with a drawstring. A memory bag, she called it, to hold my memories. Fingering the rough bag, I had remembered the angry duck with the mottled yellow bill who nipped me. I had been stroking his papery feathers when he curved his neck, his beady eye on my hand. His bill had razor edges, and the bite raised a blood blister on my finger. So, memory bag in hand, I entered the duck pen, stepped around the piles of slimy duck poop, and, keeping a wary eye on the duck, collected dropped feathers. Shaking off the powdery dirt, I inserted the blood-tipped quills in the bag and drew the string around the poking feathers, a memory to remind me that what seemed beautiful could draw blood.

The dauphine had lectured me on my duty to take up the responsibility of my life. Too late, he claimed, for him to teach me. But how could anything be too late when time itself wonked around so badly? And I'd be damned if I needed the dauphine to teach me how to get my shit together. After all, I had the city for that.

I sat cross-legged.

I opened my palms on my knees.

I closed my eyes.

The sounds and smells of New Orleans flowed around me.

I let my past rise and enclose me like the iron bars it was. In my mind, I picked at the iron's flaking rust. Sunbeams cut through dust motes. I screamed and shook the bars, helpless. Throwing myself onto the dirt floor, I cursed the universe. Suddenly, I was looking down at my tantrum, clocking my immature reaction. Who was this child with no agency, no ability to change her circumstances, and where had I gone? I rolled onto my back, still inside my cage, but my breathing calmed.

I couldn't keep running. All I had accomplished was to drag my flaws into my new world. Personify them in my grannies, even. I flashed back to the night we had all slept under one roof in my apartment. I had circled through the apartment and gazed at my sleeping ancestors, noting how they resembled my grannies, how they differed, fixing them in my memory, bathing myself in their love. But love isn't enough. The most basic psychologist could tell you trauma only healed when it was faced.

Gathering my focus, I remembered the smell of unripe green pecan hulls. My aching cheekbone. The brush of his hand against the bare skin at my waist. The instinctive shove of my elbow. The mushy noise of the obelisk entering his back. Where in all that was any fault of mine?

It was so simple, really. It only felt confusing if you accepted those with bad intent had a right to groom then rape. A right to protect his job by laying a bear trap. A right to demand romantic payment for legal services rendered. A right to willfully misread history. My boss's right to keep living his life while mine was shattered by the assault.

Still.

Regardless of the circumstances, I had done what I was not designed to do: kill another human being. Because of me, harm unto death had come to another. Which did not mean I would be scurrying over to Mississippi and turn myself in for killing Trent. The system was still weighted against me. I just had to forgive the universe for putting me in a position where violence invaded my life. Most important, unlike my grannies, I must move on.

The iron bars collapsed.

Clarity walked through the opening.

Ancient Chartres decree the Royal Dauphine drink Burgundy while seated on the Rampart of the castle until St. Claude rises from the dead, again.

We had identified Chartres. The burgundy. The castle's rampart. St. Claude. We thought we'd identified the dauphine. But the rhyme said the royal dauphine.

To hear St. Claude and the dauphine and Grande Red describe the moment of their abduction forward in time, Grande Red was hysterical at the mounting pressure: Abdicate or die. The dauphine was staring at the guillotine intended for him. The king had abdicated his crown and stood wringing his hands. But if he had already abdicated, the street in my rhyme wouldn't have been the royal dauphine. It would have been the royal king.

Brushing off my butt, I stood.

St. Claude shimmered into the air, kicking up a small dust eddy. "Etoile."

"Yes, Saint?"

"You got into a fight with the Queen Mother's collaborator?"

"He got into a fight with us. He died," I added before he could ask in his accusing tone. "Not before he told us your deal with Grande Red. You help secure the dauphine on the throne, she invests you as head of the Church in France."

When you realize everyone is lying, it releases your moral obligation to tell the truth.

"And you believe that dribble?"

"It's drivel."

"As I said."

"No, you said 'dribble,' which is a small trickle of water."

It made me wonder if my made-up mind was already erasing the saint.

"You wanted to protect the Church," I said. "Grande Red wanted to retain her power. The dauphine, well, he wanted to stay the handsome, party-loving prince. You claimed you wanted to fix the present, when really y'all just wanted to return to the past. Every one of you wanted to go back in time to before the abdication when you were safe. It's been hard to see because you came forward to go backward. It just postpones the inevitable, but that's what we do. I can't blame you. I wanted the exact same thing, to return to the time when I felt safe. Of course, that's why I gave the desire to y'all. But it's totally misdirected. No matter what we see blasting toward us, backward is not a goal. We can't go there."

It tore at my heart, I can't lie. Why did life always snatch away what we loved? The only innocents in all this, my grannies, who happily joined my quest simply because I wanted them to—once it was over, I would lose them again. Who would I love then? The barista at Bywater Coffee, who curved a slow smile as he handed me a perfectly decorated latte?

Who knows, but I'd figure it out. After all, I had dreamed up this whole fantasy.

Suddenly, the castle rose in the distance. Behind it, the church steeple pointed like a child's finger first noticing stars.

My grannies might have refused to let me find my own spot in life, but I'd outsmarted them. Who had no agency? I'd created my own world.

I strode down the street, snapping my fingers. At the end of each snap, flames shot from my thumb.

Bigmama appeared. Elfy. Tip-Top.

Then, with one big magical fart, the rest of them arrived.

St. Claude. Grande Red with the writing desk tucked under her arm. The three minions. The dauphine. The collective descending figments of my imagination lined up in front of the castle like a high school cast of *Our Town*.

Part IX

Battle

Chapter 63

I had believed myself in charge of this nonsense, but turned out I'd been manipulated by master puppeteers.

"This is my vision, okay? Mine. Have you ever in your life had a dream where you weren't the star?" I addressed the group. "No. That's not the way it works. This is my story. Etoile, the star. You all are secondary characters in my vision. I'm the hero. Ha, ha. The shero."

Grande Red rolled her eyes.

"BTW, dreams segue all the damn time. One minute you're climbing a rocky mountain, then before you know it, you're wallowing on a float in a gorgeous Caribbean swimming pool. Get ready, Claude, baby—I don't want you to be seasick."

"You warn me?" Heat crept into his cheeks.

"This castle?" I waved my hand at the mirage of the castle, and its rampart melted like spaghetti in boiling water. "Gone."

St. Claude popped his eyes at the disappeared castle. "Etoile, that is unseemly—"

"If you want to make the rules, get your own vision."

"I hereby remove the approval of the Bywater." He swirled his arm like a wizard. "We no longer cooperate with you."

The silver leaves of the Maple fluttered, but they did that all the time. Otherwise, there was no indication the Bywater gave a damn about Claude, one way or the other.

"Minions, be gone." I looked each of the red demons in the eye and tapped the air three times. The red-caped women, one by one, evaporated. But before tall Gwendolyn disappeared, a rubbery mask slipped off, revealing the wattle-face of the waiter. Grimacing, she smoked away, the piggy minion at her side squealing all the way home.

"Cool." I rubbed my palms then shook my fingers, gearing up.

Good call.

Grande Red dropped her writing desk and charged me.

Nails out, she clawed the air. I waved my hands to the side like a Tai Chi master, and she skittered horizontally, her lace boots tappy-tapping down the sidewalk. She blammed into St. Claude who caught her in his arms. His robe twirled as he spun her around.

The momentum petered out, but they continued to swirl. His robe billowed, her dress rustled. Their gazes locked, ice skater style.

I do believe they had made their choice. Maybe knowing they ended life together eased the decision. No need to go backward when the future was so bright.

With one last swirl, they were gone. A seed pearl bounced on the concrete.

I stepped backward into the middle of the street, girding my loins. The forever birds dipped and shrieked. On the river, the calliope played its tune: "Oh, when the moon turns red with blood..."

I believed the Bywater would help me if it could, but I had to give it what it desired. If I just concentrated...

My red knight jumper and sword disappeared. I stood on

the sidewalk in bra and panties in front of the vacant lot. Who cared? Every new skill carried a hiccup or two.

Tip-Top walked forward, her jacket outstretched. She guided my arms into the sleeves while Elfy arranged her shawl around my waist. Bigmama tied it all together with her sash, which caused her cudgel to fall to the sidewalk.

Tip-Top stared at her unarmed, generational nemesis. Her long fingers wandered to the hilt of her knife as she glanced at Elfy. Irrational or not, both blamed Bigmama for their deaths. Surely they sensed this time together was coming to an end. Any chance for revenge was about to literally evaporate. If my adventure ended with my grannies slaughtering each other, that would be a horrible, total failure.

Elfy's delicate palm searched the folds of her skirt. She drew her pistol.

And dropped it on the sidewalk next to the cudgel.

Tip-Top did the same with her knife.

"It's not good enough," I said.

They all stared at me.

Who was I to lecture these women? But at least I had admitted killing my boss wasn't the best thing that happened in my life. My grannies had squirreled around and done no such of a thing. Because of that, killing defined their lives. They would never heal unless they put a little more effort into it.

"Listen." I slicked my own palms against my skull. "I really appreciate what you did for me when I was a pitiful kid, but where in all of your teachings was one story of forgiveness?"

I raised my hand, halting the objections. "Not forgiving the assholes who attacked you. Forgiving the universe for asking that of you. If you just keep saying, 'I didn't do anything wrong, it was forced upon me, I had no other choice,' that loop will never stop digging ruts in your brain. You've got to do something different. Otherwise, we wind up with generations and generations spending all our mental energy justifying killing, instead of, I don't know, inventing a mechanical reaper."

"A what?" Tip-Top asked.

"Quit just stabbing holes and use your proficiency with machines to create something new." I turned to Bigmama. "Take your notes from that journal and turn them into something sacred. And you, Elfy. The house is clean, already. Use the fine china. Give a party. You're safe, your life is safe. Be happy."

"The child advises. It's time for us to go."

Without taking her gaze from me, Bigmama laid her palms out to her sisters. Elfy took one hand, Tippy the other. As one, they gathered in a circle. These women, who held more in common than any three women in the universe, finally found their affinity. They had loves in their own lives, and they needed to get busy pursuing them. After all, who knew how long the dead were given for being dead. None of them said a word. With their constant advising silenced, I was on my own. I liked it.

"You were brilliant," I whispered.

Their circling began slow then gained speed. Each allowed the other their dignity. Elfy never insisting Bigmama skip, Tip-Top never stomping on Elfy's delicate foot. No matter the beginning of their time together, it was ending in unity, and that was all that mattered.

"Etoile!" "Etoile!" "Etoile!" they cried. "Goodbye, my love." "Take care, you." "Keep in touch, child."

Like a reverse tornado, they rose. Wide at the bottom, narrowing at the top until their faces were wide-eyed close, grinning at each other like polecats. The years of animosity transformed into the most agile love. Performing a perfect over-the-arm pretzel, they twisted back-to-back, raised their hands in triumph and slowly spun so each could blow me a kiss.

"Love you." "Love you." "Love you."

In a black haze, their arms became wings, and they swooped away.

Which left me and the dauphine on the sidewalk, awkward together.

Chapter 64

Gently, the dauphine unclasped his cape and laid it on my shoulders, as if everyone in my orbit thought I was a kid unable to dress myself.

"How do you reconcile hate with accidental violence?" I asked, adjusting the cape. "I mean, when someone you hate dies at your hands, but his death was a puredee accident?"

"How do you reconcile an innocent remark with deadly consequences no child could foresee?" he answered.

Or, as with Bigmama, how do you live with shooting the one you love because you were doggedly following his instructions to forget him? Or Elfy, her will to preserve her family so strong she didn't brake until it was too late and flying shrapnel pierced her family? Or Tip-Top, when good old-fashioned self-defense was the handmaiden to revenge, like my whisperings into the ear of my rapist boss.

"I wanted my boss to die. Even if I wasn't intending it at that exact moment, I truly wanted him dead." I shuffled alongside the dauphine and, halting, kicked a semi-deflated soccer ball into the gutter. "Is that why I worry the law would find me guilty? Because I was glad?"

"This you ask of one who is above the law?"

I tested my new relationship with non-guilt and found it gone. "If only we didn't have to go through hell to get to heaven."

"Good luck with that. Even Jesus had to descend."

Our steps had brought us to the grassy edge of the castle's former home. No Tardis, no hot air balloon. No way home.

"You wanna stay?" I asked.

He turned to me. "Do you?"

Did I? Stay in this city where the corner laundry graciously offered Free Dryers Midnight to Sunrise. Where video poker happily resided in the donut shop, and the best po'boys were found in strip centers. Where purple was a normal color to paint your house. Where tattoo addiction and professional funeral dancers were real things, billboard lawyers were celebrities, and every bridge had at least two secret names. Where direction was a joke, and time a magician's triangle. Where anyone could be anything, but most importantly, exactly the thing they were meant to be.

Love swelled in my chest and whispered, *Etoile, this is your life. Love it with all your might, and never worry about it loving you back.*

"I'm gonna stay." I laid my sneaker next to his silken slipper. "Wanna stay with?"

He looped his arm through mine. His touch was cool as marble, but I chose not to dwell on what that said about the living/dead status of my new crush. "Those of us who had to defeat a dragon to arrive in this city are the ones that love it best."

"Not me." I tightened his grip on my arm. "I had to give CPR to a dying blowfish. I puffed too hard. It exploded. Splatted fish guts all over my face."

"You think the dragon was my only task?" He smiled down

at me. "That seems to be a recurring mistake of yours. Assuming the tiny part you have discerned constitutes the entire picture. And I gather you have discerned something important."

"You, my grannies, y'all helped me see my way through some traumatic events in my life. I won't let that unhappiness decide my future anymore."

I was afraid to ask him what he had learned during his time in New Orleans, not wanting to bring up the subject of his relationship with his mother.

But he told me anyway.

"As you would so eloquently say, shit gets real here, real fast."

"Is that bad?" I asked.

"Sometimes." He nudged my shoe with the edge of his slipper. "Other times, it's quite good."

I bumped his hip with mine, which knocked him a smidgen off balance and caused him to lift one foot and plant it on the castle's vacant lot.

He wobbled, a startled look on his face. A force was sucking at him, pulling him away from me.

"What are you doing?" I yelled into the space where the nonexistent castle had been. The asshole castle I thought was my friend, trying to rob me of my new-found love. Or was the castle only doing what the wayward prince wanted?

"Are you leaving me?" I asked. "Are you leaving us?"

"I do not leave of my own accord." The dauphine struggled to keep his arm looped through mine, but he was slowly sliding away.

Panicking, I yanked, trying to wrest him back to me, then realizing the folly of tugging on Superman's cape, I stepped onto the lot with him.

Chapter 65

The dauphine and I were together, but who knew where we were. The place sparkled, as if we were inside a starburst of a firecracker but with no heat. Outside of our bubble, the Bywater went about its daily business.

I took a step toward the dauphine, who looked the same but different.

"Is that you, Louis?"

"Etoile, *c'est moi*," he said, calm as the beautiful October day around us. He took a step toward me. "Is it you?"

"Louis, *c'est moi*." I grasped his fingers, and the castle, or whatever it was, didn't repel me. Instead, it seemed to draw me forward, as if encouraging the next step, one the dauphine and I had to take together.

I intertwined my fingers with his, and holding our arms in the same jitterbug dance my ancestral grannies had done, I bumped his chest.

Except I didn't bounce off.

I walked directly into his chest.

The light show around us sparked, emitting a current that swept over me, encasing us. That's what it felt like. We were encased in this space together. A second pulse of current, and I lost any sense of being separate from the dauphine. I was a surgeon's hand shoved inside a latex glove, a thin layer of not me encasing very much me.

I was enjoying the weirdness of it when something shifted. A warmth washed over me like the light that throbs into the eyes of rom-com stars when they realize they're in love. The melting spread from my heart to my bones, which became flexible as pool noodles and then gave up even that. I was floating inside my chrysalis, my innards wiggling inside me. And outside me, too, because me had become a relative term.

Then pop! The glove snapped off. The latex peeled away, and my water-puckered skin lay bare.

As did his.

Skin, I'm saying. Real skin and, from the looks of it, real throbbing muscles. I reached out and touched the vein at his temple. Warm. My very own totally naked Pinocchio man.

"What did you do?" I asked, astounded.

"Nothing." He touched my temple, as if we had created a new love language. "I didn't do anything. We did."

"It's all good then?" I kept my voice calm while forcing myself not to plaster my naked body against his. "We're actual, normal people?"

"Normal?" His mouth curved into a smile. "I certainly hope not."

"There's gonna be a lot of questions, you know." I retook his hand.

"Let the games begin," he said, intertwining our arms. Together but separate. His world, my world, our world, everyone's world.

"Life is real," I replied. "Finally."

At that moment, the troupe of naked bicyclists that haunted the Bywater pedaled by, led by the Godzilla bike.

With royal aplomb, I waved off the fake chartres that no longer defined my life, and arm in arm, the last dauphine and I left the non-castle on Rampart to join the parade on St. Claude Avenue where our naked be-hinds shone rosy as burgundy in the sun.

I swear I heard the Bywater snicker.

Acknowledgments

I want to thank the writers in my writing group: Blake Burr, Randy Mackin, Rebecca Wasson, and Wes Hutcheson. Also, Latoya Taylor, an early reader, and Cindy Bryan, my editor at Literary Wanderlust, without whom the story would never have become professionally presentable. I thank Literary Wanderlust Editor in Chief Susan Brooks who believed in the story enough to make it alive in the world.

These folks are the tip of a two-decade writing career iceberg. Over those years, I've had encouragement, support, guidance, mentoring, companionship, and the incredible gift of time from hundreds of writers, editors, mentors, teachers, readers, friends, family, acquaintances, and strangers. I thank each one of them. I particularly thank my husband Tom who has graciously supported me in every thing in every way and reads every blog post I write. Too many who supported me in my writing journey are no longer with us. I bow my head in gratitude to them. Oh, and I thank Evangeline the Extraordinary who insisted we lay up in the bed while writing this book.

To keep up with Etoile and my other writing escapades, please visit www.ellenmorrisprewitt.com where you can sign up for the newsletter to get the latest or just take a look around. Thank you for joining me on this journey. Without companions, we are surely lost.

About the Author

Ellen Morris Prewit is an award-winning author who weaves her Southern life—and family secrets—into her fiction. The humorous stories in her audio collection, *Cain't Do Nothing with Love*, have been downloaded over 50,000 times worldwide; the collection won the CIPA EVVY Audio Book Award. Her stories have twice been nominated for the Pushcart Prize; one story received an Special Mention. She's a former lawyer and obsessive swimmer. She loves hand-sewing, Godzilla, beignets with café au lait, and leading writing groups. She's a former Peter Taylor Fellow and currently serves as Writer-in-Residence at 100 Men Hall, an iconic Mississippi Blues site. She's been extensively published, including in Luna Station Quarterly, Porchlight: A Journal of Southern Literature, Gulf Coast, Unleash Lit, Image, Barrelhouse, Brevity, Arkansas Review, and EAP the Magazine. She splits her time between Memphis, the Gulf Coast, and New Orleans where she (and her husband and her dog...and her house) can frequently be found in costume. Check out her writing journey at

EllenMorrisPrewitt.com. *When We Were Murderous Time-Traveling Women* is her first traditionally-published novel.

If you liked what you read, please consider offering a review on your favorite review site—it really helps get the word out. Thank you!

https://writing.exchange/@ellenmorrisprewitt

Instagram @VEMPhaha

www.ingramcontent.com/pod-product-compliance
Lightning Source LLC
LaVergne TN
LVHW040043080526
838202LV00045B/3468